CHINA ROCK

CHINA ROCK

Laura Kelly Robb

Mark House Publishing

Seattle

Mark House Publishing

P.O. Box 47409

Seattle, WA 98146

First Mark House Publishing perfect bound edition April, 2013

For information about special discounts for bulk purchases, please contact Sales at 206–660–6982.

To book a live event with the author, contact Speakers at 206–660–6982 or go to Contact at www.markhousepublishing.com.

Cover art by Carol Aust: http://www.carolaust.com/

The logo for Mark House Publishing was designed by Patrick Zeller (pzeller@pzrider.com).

Manufactured in the United States of America

ISBN: 978-0-9889496-0-7

For
Paul and John,
brothers still

One

Island Beauty

The water was a fact of life on our dank island, more a part of us than the far and clouded sky. Its icy, homicidal currents could not be compared to the surface of a favorite swimming hole. It was a rough companion. When the wind blew in and the waves kicked up, summer or winter, we seemed like we lived at the door to the north. The water was our back yard, a border between home and afar, a spoiled child of nature whose tantrums scared us. It was Pop's route to ruin and it sometimes was our meal ticket.

It's also why those two bodies were found the way they were on Beacon Beach. One of the poor souls had his arms wrapped around the other's back and she was lodged against his chest, her arms tied around his hips, their ankles bound together. Both Chinese, they seemed to have fallen in the water alive and held on to each other for warmth. It would only have taken a few moments for them to freeze into their death position.

If Pop had come back that day, there's no doubt he would have said something cruel. Two dead people might be luckier than him, he'd say, luckier than him with his seven children, none of them too bright.

Listen to me, making up hard talk from my father, as if I didn't hear enough fresh from his own mouth.

Pop could be a mean kind of man, and now I see all sorts of reasons for it. Like the ruinous power of drink, and the way fish prices would bounce from bad to good to bad again without a whisper of a warning. The Depression had made even the kindest of men feel hard-edged at times, and Pop was not the kindest of men. But we didn't need an explanation, we needed to know how to get out of the way or fight back.

That day he would have probably laughed and called to Sarah, asking her why she didn't go for a swim with her beau, Mason, since it had turned out so romantic for those two Chinese. Sarah, who is two years older than me—and the oldest of all us seven children—would have made some ugly comment in reply, but under her breath so no one but I could hear. His attention would work on us that way. Pop could make us squirm inside and at the same time determined not to let people know we were squirming.

"Don't worry, I can think of better ways to escape the likes of you," I might have heard her say. Her mouth was wide and fearless, her even white teeth small perfect barriers.

Pop wasn't all bad. For example, he was mean to everyone equally. There were no favorites and even Belinda (whom we call Tinker for short), caught as many of his nasty gusts of anger as Sarah and any of us five boys.

After Sarah, there was me, August, the oldest boy, and just sixteen when the bodies turned up; then Jim, Howard, Crayton and Jonathan, spaced out at one, two and three-year intervals. Tinker was the youngest—a tender afterthought, as Momma described her—just three years old. Momma called us her "chain of pearls." But Pop, whose faith in Roosevelt's New Deal was being tested almost daily, saw us, I think, as just a chain around his neck.

Another good thing about Pop—well, maybe not good, but predictable, and predictable is what you want to hold onto when you are dealing with a genius for the surprise attack—was his clothing. He liked to be clean and properly dressed. Pop worked on the fishing boats, but not because he was the brawny sort who cast and drew the nets, enjoying the smell of fish and brine. He was a wiry, straight-backed man who knew how to calculate the winds and the currents to extrapolate a ship's course. He kept himself in the pilothouse during his ventures at sea with the tattered San Juan fishing fleet and he dressed the part of the well-paid navigator whenever he could on land.

His few prized possessions—a suede belt, soft leather dress shoes, monogrammed handkerchiefs, and a pair of cuff links that glowed with gold—were guarded in his bedroom. These items were the few souvenirs he had rescued from his former life, now shipwrecked against the shoals of family responsibilities and the Depression.

One more thing about Pop, and then I will have exhausted my list of his more pleasant aspects, was his wit. Sometimes rough men strike out at their children oafishly. They're like bulls taunted by a matador, and they charge at anything that comes close or stays still long enough to take a hit. Pop was not this type. It was as though he was the matador, taunting everyone with his wit and the sword of sarcasm hidden within its folds.

He could make you laugh despite yourself, despite your knowing that you'd be tomorrow's target. He made us tough and carefree that way. Unless you were just tough, like our brother Howard, and then you'd need to set something on fire every once in a while.

Take, for example, how Pop dealt with Sarah's male friends. On Sundays, Pop was sure to be home in the early afternoon when Sarah's ever-hopeful suitors would come to apply for her attentions. Sarah had early on given up trying to protect them from his barbs. I guess she reasoned she was worth his satire, since she had raven black hair and huge eyes to match, and skin so soft and rosy you thought she had never worked a day.

One Sunday in the courting season, which was pretty much all year round ever since Sarah had turned sixteen, a knock sounded at the door. Pop opened up, took a look at the hardy spirit perched unflinching on the step, and sighed audibly, letting his hand flutter over to his heart.

"My word." He closed his eyes a moment and breathed in deeply before continuing. "Sarah has started up her charity work again." Now he sighed, as if resigned to his daughter's overgenerous heart.

"Ah, my boy," he said, reaching out a sympathetic hand, "and what is your disease called?"

My brother Jim and I stood in the living room, behind the door, laughing as the pretender to my sister's heart stammered his way through the introduction. My only excuse for laughing along with Pop was that the suitors didn't care. They came back again no matter what Pop said. Such was the power of Sarah's approval.

Pop tried harder to scare off the suitors that threatened to become household fixtures. Mason Burke had been the longest lasting of her beaus, and he particularly irritated Pop, mainly because he worked on a fishing boat and actually touched the fish.

Mason was over six feet and must have weighed one eighty, maybe one hundred and ninety pounds. His hands and arms were beefy, and his neck came out to meet his collar like a wave hitting a sea wall and splashing over the edge.

Mason's size would have perhaps been less noticeable in Pop's eyes if he had tended to his hair or his clothes with more love of detail. But with tufts of wavy hair flying in the breeze, shoes scuffed out of their original color, and buttons hanging by a thread from straining cuffs, Mason in his Sunday best looked like a cabbage that had overgrown its garden patch.

Pop opened the door the third Sunday that Mason called on Sarah. He had planned to take my sister for a walk to town to buy an ice cream. As the door glided open, Pop's face twisted in pain. He staggered back and called out sharply, "Saints alive! Catherine! Kate!"

Momma heard the call and dropped the ceramic cup she was using to rinse Tinker in the tub in the kitchen. She swept up Tinker in a towel, and ran for the front door. Tinker, too astonished to cry out, perched in Mama's arms, her naked behind drooping out below the covering.

Momma found Pop, leaning against the banister of the front stairs, with his head resting on his folded arms, acting as if he could barely catch his breath.

"What is it, Ed?" Momma's voice tried to be calm but it came out scared and urgent.

"Get a priest," Pop gulped.

Momma stood rooted to the floor, and her wide frame supported the slippery Tinker comfortably on one hip. Until then, she had thought that a priest would be invited to enter her husband's house only in the case of death, his death, and even then, Edward Mohan might find a way to stop God's representative on earth from trespassing on his property. She looked uncomprehendingly at Pop.

He slowly raised his head and waved in Mason's direction.

"Get a priest," he repeated. "Can't you see that mortal sin is here?"

Momma spent her exasperation on Tinker. She seized the corner of the towel, pulled it up to Tinker's head and began to rub her curls with the energy of a shoeshine boy looking for a nickel tip. By this time the towel was wrapped so tightly around the wrong end of Tinker's pink, washed body, her arms were pinned inside and she had no choice but to take the buffeting.

Pop stood straight again, and without so much as an "excuse me," and certainly without meeting the gaze of his agitated wife, he returned to his chair in the living room, giving Mason a final top-to-bottom dismissive glance as he passed.

Mason seemed relieved to be the butt of the joke, and later he told me he thought it meant that Pop, in his own way, was accepting him into our household.

I let Mason hang on to that interpretation as long as he liked, even though I knew it to be dead wrong. Indeed, Pop didn't completely accept his own sons and daughters into his household, let alone the occasional visitor and least likely, would he recognize his own heart.

Sarah was on the cusp of eighteen, I was sixteen, and Jim and Crayton were fifteen and ten that day when half the island hiked or bicycled or horseback rode over to Beacon Beach to see the gruesome spectacle of the lonesome Chinese corpses. We had something awful to tell Pop – a story of dread – of how these foreign strangers came to rest on our island. What would he say? Could he explain something about the sea that washed them ashore? Could he make the dark details a thing of darker wit?

Any calamity in the waters around our island was unsettling. If Pop mocked our fears, especially if he mocked our fears, he might contain our anxious curiosity. It wasn't that he guided us. It was more that he baited us into being strong. Sarah searched for a way to excise herself from the fabric of the family. Dreamy, winsome Jim, and scrappy Crayton, had felt the sting of his disapproval. Howard was a package of wild impulse. And me, I was wondering if I could do better than Pop, and hoping I wouldn't do worse. We all expected, in our own ways, to hear him tell us something brave from the wider world. We expected him to bully us into dismissing the sight of abandoned corpses.

He would return home that night from the sea, we thought. But he didn't.

Two

Jim and Crayton

By that summer of 1936, my brother Jim's voice had deepened, although unexpected warbling would occasionally ambush his masculine dignity. Crayton was nothing but a cub scrambling to keep up with Jim's pace. Honestly, they were an unlikely pair but as happens in some families, the brother or sister that is closest in age to you is not always the one you see eye to eye with. Maybe it's because you have to share clothes, or maybe because you both wanted your mama's attention at the same time. Now this rule didn't exactly hold for Sarah and me. We were friends without even talking about it. Maybe it was because being so different from each other, we never got in each other's way.

But the pattern held for Jim and Crayton. They had Howard between them but they preferred to leapfrog the closer brother to spend time with each other. Now someone watching our family from the outside might think what I'm saying is odd. To any islanders who knew us, it was Jim, Howard and I who seemed cut from the same cloth: tall, long-limbed fellows with strong chins and black shocks of thick hair. We were the potential state champions that coaches while away their winters dreaming of. Howard was, at thirteen years old, already developing a powerful chest, and the thing that he did with no effort and a great deal of grace was hit a baseball.

The same design and proportions that Howard had were draped over Jim's frame, but here's where appearances deceived. Jim, even with his ample shoulders and generous reach, didn't care for sports though once in a while just to tease Howard he would pitch him some fast ones. Howard would beg him to join his team, if only for one Sunday afternoon game. But as much as Howard loved sports, Jim loved books. Jim would rather find a corner to sit and read, a notion that Howard found unbearably useless.

As you might have guessed, Crayton's inclinations were like Jim's. As soon as Crayton learned to be quiet through enough hours of reading, Jim would let him come along on his Sunday reading marathons. All Crayton would need was a pencil and paper, and as Jim read, Crayton would sketch.

One of their favorite spots was a twenty-by-twenty shed that sat up on Monument Hill and had a view of the San Juan Straits. The shed had survived the farmhouse that burned down years before, so stood unused but handy to a well-worn path up the hill. From this lookout they could see tumultuous growths of pine and cedar reigning over the view of vast blue green waters outlined by rocky shores.

The shed had an overhang on its south side so Jim and Crayton could look down on the Straits but still be shielded from most winds and all the rain. If the air was still and sunshine was available, they would climb on the windowsill, get a toehold in the broken cedar shingles, and clamber up to the roof. Jim drank in Mark Twain and Robert Louis Stevenson while Crayton watched hawks and eagles float on air currents as lazily as if they had been napping. They would spend hours on the roof, and more than once the imprint of the shingles could still be seen on Jim's back when he took his shirt off for bed.

Down below the shed, rabbits and deer happened by. Occasionally a snake would slither from underneath the shed, up the wall and blithely onto the crumbling roof. Crayton loved those moments because he could match the snake's immobility with his own calm focus. Crayton would sit perfectly still, memorizing the pattern on the snake's back and the slit of its mouth. Although Jim professed an abiding fear of all reptiles, he would point with pride to the details in Crayton's drawings such as the grit in the eye of the snake and the coloration of the tip of its tail.

Jim admitted that as a reflex he would touch Crayton's drawings to see if the things would crawl off the page.

Jim admired Crayton's drawings and would try some himself but couldn't come close to the accuracy of Crayton's pencil. They began to save the best ones, and after school, or during the tawny early evenings of spring, together they would consult the natural history books at the San Juan County library.

At the thick oak tables of the modest library, Jim and Crayton lived a life larger than our constrained home could permit. From the stacks they pulled the leather-bound references full of the tones and shapes of a world so grand that even Pop could not discredit it. Through a carefully guarded collection of colored lithographs, they traveled across the mountains of the Northwest and Canada as intrepid naturalists.

Crayton leafed through books of exotic birds, plants that eat insects and lizards that walk on water. Meanwhile Jim, from tomes on Washington, Idaho, and British Columbia, searched out a match for Crayton's latest drawing. In his most careful penmanship, Jim would write a summary of the habits and the surroundings of the sketched creature. Many afternoons after school Jim and Crayton wouldn't stop until the library closed, and then they faced the late hike back home.

A walk home from the library was a long haul by anyone's standards. But it was particularly strenuous for Crayton, who just wasn't built like most of us Mohans.

Crayton had the short, punky body of a sea sponge. He was shapeless, not in a fatty way, but a boneless, honeycomb way. I remember when he was tiny we would rearrange him as he napped in his bassinet, and each time we moved him he would look like a different baby. Since it wasn't really clear where his arm met his shoulder or his backside turned into his leg, Momma gave up trying to fit his clothes and kept him together instead with straps and buttons.

Sometimes on those walks from the library, Crayton would struggle so hard to keep up that Jim, bored with his slow pace, would hitch him up on his back and carry him a good part of the three miles from town to our home.

One day, right when May had turned into June and June was turning into summer, Jim and Crayton finished the thirtieth page of sketches and descriptions. The librarian, Miss Paletto, who had taken some notice of their hard work, asked them what they thought they would do with their burgeoning collection. Jim answered that he wanted to keep them, like you keep a book, to browse and remember sometimes.

Miss Paletto's eyes widened suddenly and she turned on her heels, disappearing into her small office.

"Now you've done it," Crayton sighed.

"What? Done what?" Jim was baffled.

"You made her angry, talking about a book! We've got a pile of scratchings and you go and call it a book! You've got all the sense of a beheaded chicken."

Miss Paletto returned with sharp, hurried steps, and a sheet of paper firmly grasped in her hand.

A note to Momma, thought Crayton, *explaining why we should be given more chores at home to keep us from disturbing library personnel.*

"You boys might like to see this announcement," Miss Paletto

23

chirped pleasantly. Crayton's shoulders relaxed back down into his rounded back.

The announcement was set in small, close type and looked to Crayton like the instructions that came with the syrup of ipecac that Momma insisted on using to treat their ailments. But Jim scanned it quickly and looked at Miss Paletto with amazement.

"Does this mean us?" asked Jim.

"Of course it means you," smiled the librarian. "It says 'writers of any age' can enter a manuscript. The prizes are modest but more importantly..."

Crayton wholly forgot his manners and interrupted with a start and a grunt.

"Prizes? Prizes? Where does it say prizes?"

"Here," offered Jim, using his most courteous tone for the sake of Miss Paletto. "Let this headless fowl read it to you."

Jim read:

FIRST BOOK CONTEST

All comers of all ages are invited to submit a first book, written in correct English, the pages bound and numbered, for consideration by the jury of the University of Washington Writer's Club New Publications Contest.

Entries in the five areas of fiction, poetry, scientific study, travel and social criticism will be judged separately.

Each entry must be original and must be the first book written in any area by the cited author or authors.

Prizes will be awarded based on the content and readability of the material, as well as accuracy in the cases of the non-fiction categories. First, second and third prizes will be awarded in each category. First prizes: $100; second prizes: $50; third prizes: $25.

Delivery of the manuscripts to be considered must be made to the Writer's Club by July 1, 1936.

Crayton jumped from his chair, reaching across Jim to grab the sheet of information, but Jim quickly held it high out of his brother's excited reach.

"I just want to crumple that thing, Jim. Let me have it," begged Crayton.

"What is wrong with your brother?" Miss Paletto enunciated in a low tone.

"He's not been himself since the operation."

"What operation?" she inquired sympathetically.

"I believe they removed his brain," Jim said, glaring at Crayton.

"Can't you see?" Crayton said, his mouth bunched up into an angry pout. "Our writings are as good as any. What does it matter if they're not bound?"

"The rules aren't ours, Crayton," answered Jim sternly. "And they surely are not Miss Paletto's fault."

"Sorry, Miss Paletto," said Crayton as he flopped heavily back into his chair.

"I can appreciate your chagrin, Crayton. But I have an idea about how to prepare your manuscript."

Miss Paletto explained that three times a year she sent out old books to Seattle to be rebound, and if they wanted, she could get their pages bound by the same company. For four dollars, the sheets of words and drawings would come back with the protection of back and front hard covers.

Jim said that was a fine idea, but Crayton rubbed his chin, looked carefully at Miss Paletto, and asked if she didn't think four dollars was a bit steep for just thirty pages. While Crayton's body may have been slack, and his temper immature, his brain seemed to have been lifted from a Mississippi River blackjack dealer whose demise had been no accident.

"Most books have upwards of a hundred pages, Miss Paletto", Crayton said gravely. "Why, in school, I believe there are even books with over one hundred and fifty pages."

Miss Paletto, who wasn't one to slip lightly over an unexamined fact, removed a book from the nearest shelf and flipped it to the last page.

"Aaah, two hundred and twenty-three pages, Crayton Mohan," she nodded to him. "How right you are."

She closed the book gently, returned it to the shelf, and sighed.

"All right. Three dollars and twenty-five cents. But I know they'll go no lower. Two hard covers cost a lot, no matter how few pages are sandwiched in between them."

Miss Paletto took their manuscript of lifelike drawings and careful, handwritten natural science research to be sent to Seattle upon payment of the cost of binding.

"Miss Paletto, if we win, we will pay you back double the cost of the binding," Crayton promised. Jim looked askance at his brother and then added:

"Wait, Miss Paletto. Add this please."

On a clean sheet of paper Jim carefully inscribed, *This book is dedicated to our favorite librarian, Miss Paletto.*

The young librarian took the sheet from Jim and inserted it behind the title page of their manuscript. "I'm honored, Jim," she said quietly.

Once outside, Crayton leapt on Jim's back, hollering his pleasure at striking a favorable deal with Miss Paletto, one of the island's more firm-minded citizens. Jim whirled Crayton around so that his elbows and hair flew out and he hung on with his knees.

"Imagine us with a book!" Jim whooped.

"Imagine us with one hundred dollars!" Crayton crowed again, but suddenly Jim's foot stomping came to a halt.

"Where are we going to get the three dollars and twenty-five cents?" Jim asked.

"Berries, berries, and more berries!" Crayton was nearly yelling into Jim's ear.

Jim set Crayton down with a thud. "Berries? At ten cents a flat, you'd have to pick thirty-two-and-a-half flats," reasoned Jim. "And berries won't happen until August."

"Jim, you're calculating by blackberries. I'm calculating by strawberries. Picking strawberries, we'd get thirty cents a flat and that means just less than eleven flats," Crayton answered.

"And that means convincing Mr. Dockton to let us work his fields. After the mess with you and Howard and the fire last year, I don't think that's likely."

By the time Jim and Crayton got home, the wind had gone out of their publishing sails. I heard the story just as I have told it to you, perhaps with a few extra sighs and some more regret thrown in. They sat in a heap on the bed in our crowded room and told me how beautiful a bound edition of their very own words and drawings would look. They seemed to me sadder than a fish on a hook.

"What you've got to do is visit Mr. Dockton right away," I advised Crayton. "Tell him that setting his fence on fire was probably—no, was certainly—the stupidest thing two boys could ever do. Tell him you have not touched a match, not you and not Howard, for ten months now. Tell him you'll pick for twenty-five cents a flat, to make it up to him."

"Then we'd be up to thirteen flats," said Crayton and Jim together. Their heads sunk down onto their hands, and their cheeks pushed up towards their eyelashes, and for just a moment tears appeared in the narrow slits of Crayton's eyes. Jim took a sidelong glance at Crayton, and then he straightened up his back and lifted his chin.

"We can do that! Look at these hands. These hands have picked more berries than any two hands in the San Juan Islands. Maybe any two hands in the state of Washington," Jim boasted.

I should have paused right there to wonder if this intensity would not be the seed of some irreversible disappointment, but his revived enthusiasm encouraged me.

"Yeah, and that mouth has eaten more berries than any mouth belonging to any two hands," Crayton reminded him.

"Yeah, Jim, this'll be different," I said. "We're going to have to be serious. No nibbling."

"I know. I can control myself," Jim frowned, and seemed to turn a little sour from the criticism.

Whenever his face clouded over, my judgment always slipped. I offered to help. I don't know if it was because of all the reading or all the thinking that Jim did, but he could often loosen my grasp on practicality with one baleful glance. If he sank into sadness, and his eyes went dull, my days took on a stuffy awkwardness, like when you go to a birthday party for the cake and then find out you have to sit and listen to the birthday girl play duets on the piano with her mother. Sometimes I could stave off his blueness, sometimes not. But I knew that helping him get his book bound was the only thing I could do in this situation.

If nothing else, I thought, I could make sure that Mr. Dockton and Pop didn't come to blows again as they did last year over the burned fence. Granted, the fence was pretty useless by the time Howard and Mr. Dockton had put out the fire, but it wasn't worth two grown men trying to broaden each other's noses about it.

Of course, at first Pop had been furious with Howard. He called him an idiot and took off his belt and whacked Howard on the back of his calves. Crayton, who was too young and thunderstruck at the effect of matches put to old wood to take full blame, got away with a light spanking. But that punishment had been a father's duty, Pop thought. On the other hand, Mr. Dockton had no right to insult Pop's son, so when Pop heard him call Howard a donkey's hind end, Pop sent his right fist into his nose. Pop had gone over to the strawberry farm to make amends, but came back with split knuckles, a bloody mouth, and a swollen eye. Howard stayed away from the dinner table for a week, and Pop got the tenderest treatment I'd ever seen from Momma, which, I suspect, he truly enjoyed.

So if Pop got wind that Crayton and Jim were going to Mr. Dockton to ask to be accepted back into his good graces, he'd be harder to handle than a raccoon in an outhouse. Better we should go together and get those thirteen flats, and get back home before Pop noticed we were gone.

Three

Pop

Pop took the Depression hard. He knew how to have a good time, but the way he liked to have a good time involved money, good restaurants and fine scotch, cigars, racing horses, silk ties, and a daily visit to his barber. Pop was the life of the party, and would hold the floor until two in the morning telling stories of clever characters and brushes with the law. He could deal cards like lightning, win hands, and still have everyone asking to stay in the game. He had a memory for faces and details that stood him in good stead in the taverns and speakeasies of every city he visited between his birthplace in Ireland and his last watering hole in Seattle.

Sometimes Pop would find himself in the company of several friends, Momma recounted, and a man he had not seen in a raft of years would approach, and look sideways at Pop as if to try and place him. Pop would extend his hand, squint up into the man's face as if to say "what's kept you away?" and ask about his wife and children by name.

Someone once asked Momma if Pop kept a notebook of names and stories about people. She had laughed and said no, that just like you and I might remember our address and own birthday, he could remember everything he heard, as long as it was connected to someone's face. She also said she thought he could remember the cards he held in every hand he had ever won, but that was another talent altogether and one that simply led down the wrong road.

He was a city man through and through, Momma said, probably from the first moment he put on a pair of shoes. He was born in Dublin, Ireland, and his mother, a dark-haired beauty, is pushing him in an elaborate pram towards an imposing fountain in the only surviving picture we have from his childhood. His father, who had been out of the picture and joking with the photographer that day, was supposedly a gentle, playful man who had a roving eye. He managed the deliveries for a small brewery and seemed to have friends in every corner of the city. Before Pop turned two, his father went out for a pack of cigarettes one evening and never returned. My grandmother discovered that any money they had saved was gone with him, and she had no choice but to emigrate to Pittsburgh, where an older sister had married and settled.

Once in Pittsburgh, Grandmother Mohan cleaned houses and shops, but dusted herself off well enough on Sundays to go to social gathering organized by her church, or her brother-in-law's union, or her fellow charladies, or her sister's friends. By the time Pop turned four, Grandmother Mohan was Mrs. Brennan, the wife of a Pittsburgh policeman.

Jack Brennan, Pop's stepfather, sired three daughters in quick succession. Pop was nine years old when the third arrival, Margaret, was brought home to their modest apartment in a red brick walkup on the south side of Pittsburgh. Grandmother Mohan no longer cleaned for a living, but life was still not an easy proposition. Laundry was done by hand in a cement basin, groceries were purchased daily, a coal stove was tended for heat and cooking, and potatoes and bread had the same prominence on the family menus as they did back in Dublin. But Grandmother Mohan liked to laugh, and Pop liked to entertain, so he learned to juggle and do magic tricks, and he brought home every funny story he heard to try out on his favorite audience of one, Anna Mohan Brennan.

Jack Brennan was a good policeman in that he understood when to enforce and when to look the other way. He knew that the police commissioner's loyalty was first to the political heavyweights of Pittsburgh, and then to the cause of law and order. Jack spread the word through his precinct of which candidates to support at each election, and helped in the collection and delivery of loyalty payments of local businessmen to key officials. He did not benefit from graft himself, except to keep his job, and in that way, he kept his nose clean and his life simple. He would have raised his daughters and his slight but excitable stepson in relative harmony if he had been permitted to govern his life as he saw fit, but the lamentable state of public health intervened—somewhat adversely affected by the very graft Jack Brennan tolerated.

When Pop's youngest half-sister Margaret, who had the square-cut face of a Brennan and the thin, blond hair that went with it, fell ill with tuberculosis, the family's routine ground to a halt. To care for her, Grandmother Mohan all but moved into the hospital. Surrounded by small and whimpering young patients who cried out for caresses, she soon contracted the disease herself. Within two months, she and Margaret succumbed to the pneumonia that invaded their weakened lungs.

Pop did not learn directly of his mother's death. He was twelve years old, and the stunned Jack Brennan took the three remaining children to his sister's house in the western outskirts of the city, where the hills of Pittsburgh became the mining district of Pennsylvania. He told Pop, and his sister, that the city was too infected to be safe and that he would return when his wife and child were discharged from the hospital and he could find better accommodations for all of them. Jack returned to Pittsburgh and proceeded to drink himself into a stupor at the home of whatever fellow policeman would have him. This situation might have gone on indefinitely but for the fact that two weeks after his wife and child's funeral, still drunk from melancholy and the indulgence of the night before, he walked in front of the first streetcar of the morning traffic and died instantly. A week passed before his next of kin were located, and another week after that before the full story of the deaths of Grandmother Mohan and Margaret were known to Pop.

The Policeman's League provided a small bit of income for Jack Brennan's survivors, which included Pop's half sisters, Grace and Kate Brennan, but not him, the stepson. Pop's aunt, Agnes, tried to put the best face on the situation, but Pop knew his presence was a burden that no one, least of all Agnes' overworked husband, could afford. There was some talk of turning the boy over to his mother's sister, but that aunt's own brood of six had left her literally toothless and without a crumb to spare, even on holidays. Agnes gritted her teeth and remembered that Jack would have done the same for her if the tables had been turned, and she cared for Pop as best she could.

He lasted three years in the small, coal-centered town, a place he always referred to as Hell's Outhouse, a place that was as rough as it was uncouth. What can you say, Pop would demand when we tried to poke into his youth, about a place where flatulence was cultivated as a method of communication? Pop told me one night, after he had drunk more whiskey than he needed, that "sitting and waiting for your balls to grow big enough to get you a job in an underground pit was what passed for education."

He sparred with the overgrown miners' sons at the schoolyard and ignored the sour looks of his step-uncle, waiting for a growth spurt that never came. After enough whiskers sprouted on his upper lip so he could wear long pants with a modicum of authority, he was gone back to Pittsburgh and what he anticipated as the pleasures of city life. To get himself established, he carried only his aunt's good wishes and the address of one of Jack Brennan's old friends.

Pop turned fifteen on his way out of town, and he turned into a man his first day back in Pittsburgh, or that was how he told it to Momma, and me, on occasion. He said life was handed to him on a platter, and all he had to do was learn to use the right utensils. His stepfather's policemen friends sized up Pop as a quick learner who had very little to lose. He had come out of coal mining territory with a steely eye, a taut wit, and no hesitation about letting his temper show. They steered him to a man they knew could provide opportunities for a boy who offered mind over muscle: a bar owner and horse racing enthusiast named Manny Burroughs.

Manny "loved the nags," as he put it, and for that love, he walked in the narrow lane between the sporting life and illegality. Manny thought the horses beautiful and strong, creatures out of history and mythology, who tolerated their riders and the noisy crowds for the sheer exhilaration of flying around the track spewing cinders in their wake. At the track, Manny forgot the noxious fumes of Pittsburgh and the implicit control that the sinewy tentacles of steel and banking had over every working family. Racing happened in West Virginia, and West Virginia was pure and wholesome country to Manny. The fact that a few of the people involved in the racing life did not share Manny's purity of purpose both displeased him and kept him in employment.

Manny was a sort of an unofficial public relations officer for the West Virginia tracks. He touted the races to his customers, and kept people abreast of the horses and their odds of winning. He emphasized the competitions most likely to attract good purses and lots of bets, and for trusted customers he would convey their money across the state line into the hands of bookies. West Virginia gamblers thought Manny was a rare prize since he asked only for minimal fees and the right to rub shoulders with the owners and jockeys on his visits to the races. When it was clear as water that a race had been "handled" by a jockey and Manny's friends lost their sure bets, he would not besmirch the sport with criticism. He cheered his friends with a round on the house and gabbed about the excellent qualities of thoroughbreds of note. His consistency and cordiality kept him on good terms with bookies and customers so that there were few complaints and even fewer incidences of violence, a fact that was not lost on the policemen pals of Jack Brennan. They decided that leading Pop to Manny was a good placement for a boy who nobody knew but everybody agreed should be given some kind of chance to escape the nasty luck so far visited upon him.

Pop was slight enough and smart enough to be of great use to Manny. At first, Manny subcontracted him to a track manager he knew in West Virginia. Pop was none too happy to be leaving Pittsburgh so soon after re-discovering civilized life. But something in Manny's joyful descriptions of horseracing dispelled Pop's reluctance. He rode across the West Virginia state line in the roadster of a jockey whose sophistication and billfold convinced him that mining and racing were going to be two different worlds.

With legendary speed, Pop learned to groom the horses, then exercise them, then diagnose their weaknesses and strengths and coach their jockeys accordingly. He was direct and scathing with the jockeys, which they respected, and he was Manny's eyes and ears. For the information he could bring back to Pittsburgh, each Monday and Tuesday he had off, on various horses' health, their owners' intentions, their jockeys' frustrations, and who was betting or not betting, Manny provided him, through the stable owner, with meals, a room, work clothes, and pocket cash. Manny parlayed the information into useful and remunerated hints for his customers and he used it to inform his own bets. He was also generous with thorough explanations of the mathematics of betting so that Pop learned statistics and probability better than most college graduates.

Pop began recording wins and losses of various jockeys, horses, tracks, owners, roomers and exercise boys. He paid attention to speed, weather, time of the year, and the number of races each horse had run and won, and he started to calculate correlations among the different factors so that he could make predictions for each race. He kept track of his predictions and successes until he could produce a factor of accuracy that surpassed that of anyone else he knew in the betting world. Pop shared the columns of information with Manny whenever he asked for it, but not the predictions. Manny made his own predictions, had reasonable success, and never had a suspicion that the young Mohan orphan knew more that he told. For his part, Pop was happy to lay his own bets quietly and save. Pop had few outlays, new clothes when he needed them, and a growing sense of security provided by a bank account. Pop said it was all a game for him, full of twists and turns, drama and surprise endings, success alternating with fewer and fewer failures. That is, until he turned twenty-one and too large to ride the precious racehorses, even for a warm-up lap.

"So Manny was like a second father to you?" I asked Pop one night when he was fingering a few old photos he kept.

"He was more like a teacher. Not like one of the cockamamie teachers in this hopeless town. He was a bona fide teacher who knew his trade. God help you get a job with the pitiful education you're receiving," he answered.

Manny invited Pop to Kentucky on a short junket with the stable owner, Gordy Braichs. A visit to the "birthplace of champions" during spring training was Manny's reason for living. Horse trainers showed off their new crop of thoroughbreds to potential agents and buyers with charm and plenty of whiskey. Pop said he realized he had grown heavier that spring when he was able to follow Manny and Gordy around Kentucky morning, noon and night and not fall on his face dead drunk.

Unfortunately, Gordy and Manny had noticed the growth also, and were looking in Kentucky not only for new horses but for Pop's replacement.

Manny broke the news to him gently, Pop said, like a cop breaks it to you gently that you're arrested—with a club over the head. In this case, they were loading the last horse into the wagon for the ride back when Manny gave him fifty dollars and told him to find his own way back to Pittsburgh, or wherever he was going, because the new stable boy needed his space in the truck.

"Figure it out for yourself, boy," Manny said. "You weigh one-thirty-five now."

Pop would use that line on us whenever we asked for help and he wasn't in the mood to help, which was almost always. He even used it on Jonathan, who didn't reach one-thirty-five until well past his own twenty-first birthday.

"Do I look like a country boy?" he once snapped at me when I asked him to show me how to cast a good line with my fishing pole down in the stream near our house. "Besides, you weigh one-thirty-five now. Figure it out for yourself."

Left on his own in the spring of 1913, in the middle of a flowering, grass-scented landscape, Pop said he thought of the Ireland his mother had lovingly described and that he could not remember. And he wondered if his life was simply not meant to be lived on this side of the ocean. He would go back to Dublin and surely find some remaining cousins or uncles who could start him in a new trade or at least point him to the best-outfitted horse stables where he could resume his career. He hopped a train to Pittsburgh, and booked himself passage on a freighter to London where he would find a boat to Ireland. There was a war brewing in Europe, but the Irish would be smart enough to keep clear of that kind of nonsense, he felt sure.

To give himself a little insurance for his new life, he wandered out to West Virginia a few days before his ship departed to place one last bet on a race he had calculated as a sure thing. It was the bet that ruined his life, he told me time and again. He would be a gentleman in Dublin today, he was certain of it, if it weren't for that bet. The bet that shook his world.

He won the bet and won it big. In his youthful fearlessness, he had placed his largest bet ever and came away with over two thousand dollars—a fortune for anyone, a treasure beyond belief for an unemployed man of twenty-one. Bookies encircled him, it seemed like, each aware that this bet was not one of dumb luck, and that Pop was someone they could not afford to have working for the competition. Frank Grogan made Pop the best offer of all. Pop would have a salary, an apartment in Pittsburgh, a car to drive to West Virginia, and no work but to keep his notes, make his calculations, and feed Grogan his predictions for each and every race. Ireland might be everything he had heard, Pop thought, but it could not be better than the life of leisure and horse racing. Horse racing was growing so fast all along the Atlantic coast that there would be limitless opportunities for a man of his abilities.

For the next few years of his heyday, Pop knew who prepared the best steak, who poured the best Scotch, and who was the quickest tailor in countless towns up and down the East Coast. He knew the names of all the porters who would bring him his cigar in the dining car on the innumerable train trips he took. He traveled east and west, on loan to bookies in Saratoga, Albany, Trenton, Danbury, Boston, Cincinnati and Chicago. He had his favorite hotels in every city, and even his favorite taxi drivers.

"Why didn't you get married, Pop, with all that money?" I asked him during his storytelling one drink-dampened night.

"Bah! The girls didn't want me for a husband. I was too slick and they were too smart. I was a mighty fine walk on the wild side though. Mighty fine," he chuckled.

But fortunes change, and Pop's fortunes changed with an alacrity that made his heart crack. At least, that's how I explained Pop to myself. As he told it, he had his betting system honed to a fine science.

"I could tell by who was brushing them and who was riding them and what they were eating, who would win. I liked to get a look, because a horse's coat and eyes tell more than the pedigree, but I could call races in other cities with horses I'd never seen if I just had enough of the facts. But men are never satisfied. It's not enough to win ninety percent of the time. Grogan had to win, and then rob someone blind on top of it. I should have never trusted him. I knew from the first day, just like a horse, it was in his eyes." Pop cupped his hands around the top of his head when he told me this part of the story, and let his forehead sink down toward the table.

"Grogan had to cheat. It was in his nature. Had to throw a race I could have called honestly. Had to get everyone around him in hot water. There's nothing worse than a greedy man unless it's a greedy gambling man. And gamblers are all greedy."

More than once I had plopped Pop into his bed while he continued murmuring about greedy and dangerous gamblers.

Frank Grogan told the men he was cheating—a couple of brothers from Gary, Indiana—that Pop had been part of some scheme to fix the race and had purposely miscalled it, predicting another horse as winner. He told the men where Pop was, up in New Jersey, probably fixing another race, Grogan added. Luckily, when they showed up at Pop's hotel slightly under the influence of beer and whiskey, Pop was cold sober. He locked himself in the bathroom, and while they figured out how to shoot open the lock, he went out the window, down the fire escape, and hied off to the station hours early for the train back to Pittsburgh, but just in time to hop on a freight to Michigan.

It took him weeks to zigzag across the country to San Francisco because he feared riding on the standard passenger trains, open as they were to the scrutiny of the easily compromised railroad police. He knew the two brothers from Gary would keep up their search for weeks until they became convinced he had fled the country, or until they won back some of their money.

Once in San Francisco, he had a much-reduced bank account, and a draft number. It was 1917. Pop was single, twenty-five years old, healthy but unemployed, and the United States had entered the war in Europe. His fate seemed all but inevitable, and he could imagine the weight of a knapsack on his back and the sound of exploding artillery in his ears as he sat drinking up his last dollar's worth of liquor in a San Francisco bar.

The bartender was a bashful fellow who appreciated Pop's wit. He offered Pop a few bucks to deliver some cases of Scotch to a shipping company on the wharf. When Pop walked in, he said, he was ushered into a room of several desks, some high and some low, some with stools, and all facing a large window looking out on the bay. To collect his payment for the Scotch, he was directed to a man at a spot close to the front window, and as he walked among the desks he saw each worker toiling over calculations of different kinds. Some calculated angles, others were figuring speeds, or tides, or costs of freight. Whatever their purpose, they were engaged in mathematical inquiries Pop was all too familiar with.

At the last desk before the manager's, he paused to watch a man squirming over an equation that seemed obvious to Pop.

"It goes like this, for Lord's sake," Pop exclaimed into his ear and the room went quiet. The man shoved the paper out of Pop's reach, but it was too late. The manager walked over, took a look at the sheet, verified Pop's answer and hired him on the spot.

"You'll crew to Alaska, get yourself some experience and a merchant marine license, and that'll keep you out of the draft," his new employer ordered. "After a while, you'll figure out the rest of the business and maybe get yourself a desk someday."

That contact was about as extensive as the human resources function was in those days, and Pop soon found himself sailing back and forth between San Francisco and Anchorage, sick as a dog most days, always shivering. His hands were twisted from hanging on to lines in the cold, but he was out of the range of murderous German fire.

On one trip he met Momma at a church picnic in Seattle, and on another trip he was ushered into the pilot house and asked to perform calculations in the stead of a sick navigator. On a different trip he was made ship's agent to the Alaskan import company they served. On a short two-week leave, he married Momma and bought a house. Eight months later he returned for the baptism of his first child, Sarah, who was, we were always told, a sickly, premature infant. He must have been back in Seattle in the spring of 1919, because in the winter of 1920 I was born, and by that time he was managing agent for all his company's Alaskan customers.

The war was over and Pop ached to get away from the shipping industry and ships, their incessant schedules of loadings, sailings, unloadings and return sailings. The loneliness of the long trips, the bad company of roughneck sailors, the miserable food and the sameness of dockside taverns was of no help in the humanizing of my father. He must have had a human side, however, because his children kept coming, and by necessity he continued to climb on board the freighters headed northward.

By 1929, he had made more than sixty trips, had learned seamanship, navigation, cargo loading, and salesmanship, and there were six of us kids. Pop came in and out of our Seattle home on his short breaks between voyages like a man picking his way across a puddled field. He would step over or around us, and did not tolerate smeared faces or snotty noses. If he ever picked me up, I don't remember; but I do remember his handkerchief was always pressed and clean in his breast pocket so he would use the wrinkled one out of his pants pocket to wipe us off.

He was poised to receive his desk job, and move us all down to San Francisco. Momma had taken me to the library and we borrowed books about California to get a look at what we would now call home. I imagined us walking back and forth across the Golden Gate Bridge and riding cable cars to and from school. His hard work was paying off and earning him the businessman's landlubber life he had never wanted to leave in the first place.

Of course, the October crash ruined everything. The owners of the shipping line had been speculating in bonds and real estate with the company's assets, and paychecks were the first item to disappear from their ledgers. There was talk of getting the ships out of dry dock after a year or so, but new funds never materialized, and Pop grew tired of waiting.

I remember selling pieces of furniture, and I remember we grew to hate mackerel in a hurry. We kept our dog for as long as we could, but he either slunk away to a family that would feed him, or Pop carried him off, I am not sure. When a friend of Momma's told her about cheap houses for rent in the San Juan islands, where men still found work on fishing boats, I don't remember much discussion, we just moved up from Seattle in a borrowed car. Pop found the town with the largest fishing fleet and Momma was relieved to know it had the largest Catholic parish of all the islands. Pop said that was good because it usually meant it would have the largest taverns, too, since nothing could make a man drink harder than to see a bunch of women clucking along behind a priest.

I remember thinking that I had gotten what I wished for because Pop was home more often than not, and I remember that he did not seem to see the advantage of it. I figured it would just take him some time to get to love his new life. I don't remember when I stopped waiting for that to happen.

Four

Promises

We were lucky that spring of 1936. Because the sun had shone strong in May, by June the strawberry crop bulged off the plants. Hot days made sweaty work, but at least filling up the containers with berries would be as easy as coaxing a song from a songbird.

The Saturday morning after Jim and Clayton hatched their plan, the day after school got out for the summer, Jim suggested heading down the dusty road to Mr. Dockton's big fields early in the morning, before the heat could make you feel asleep and awake at the same time. I would stay behind just long enough to distract the rest of the family from Crayton's and Jim's mission. No one could suspect for a moment that Pop's boys would stoop to work for the man who had insulted them the year before.

Sarah had left for her job at the cannery before dawn. Jonathan and Tinker were still too young to notice anybody's whereabouts but Momma's. Pop was sleeping off Friday night's socializing and probably wouldn't notice much until afternoon. But when he got up, things would have to look right. Momma would have to have a natural explanation about where everyone was, and Howard would have to believe it, too.

I started with Howard first. He was in our room, the boys' room, off the kitchen. We called it the porch because that made it sound better than it was, a dark storage area that Pop had converted to his sons' dormitory. The walls were unfinished and open to the studs. We would have been able to see through the chinks between the planks of exterior siding if it had not have been for Pop stuffing newspaper between the studs, and then tacking over it with old clothes. Some mornings my first thought as I looked through eyes open just a slit was that I was floating over the bed and until I fully awoke and regained my sense of direction, I had the pleasant sensation of flying through a plaid sky.

Howard was shining Pop's shoes, squinting to see every detail in the poor light. Sunny or not, I knew he wouldn't shine the shoes outside for fear that dust would get on them and Pop would refuse to pay him.

Howard was an enigma to me, a puzzle whose pieces kept changing in shape and number. He would come in after dinner some nights, sweaty from a game of baseball, mud deep under his fingernails, his knuckles, wrists and ankles brown from it too, and he'd fall into bed without a thought to soap and water. Yet he'd be the one to clean Pop's shoes with a glowing pride in their perfection.

Howard would hold Jonathan upside down over his back, until Jonathan either wet his pants or threatened to, an event not received kindly by Momma or Sarah. But Howard would stay up late, all the night, if needs be, on Christmas Eve, to help Momma finish the toys and sweets she was making for Jonathan and Tinker's surprise the next morning.

I guess if he could do something with his hands, he didn't stop to evaluate the worth of it, he just forged ahead and did it. Momma used to call him her Go Ahead Boy, because there was no use in trying to keep him from doing things.

I didn't have a nickname for Howard, or any other way to get closer to him, and I approached him with caution. I thought if I could just get him talking, I could find a way to keep him busy while I crept off to pick strawberries. It would have to be something that kept him so busy he wouldn't think to ask where Crayton, Jim and I had gone to.

"Hey, Howard," I started casually. "Pop's going out tonight?" I sat down on my cot. Howard and I each had our own cot because we were wild sleepers and kicked the wall or our brothers with equal lack of remorse. Crayton, Jim, and Jonathan had to cope in one bed, which was no mean feat since Jonathan was also developing flaying legs. In self defense, Crayton and Jim had taken to throwing their arms over Jonathan's limbs, and when the three of them were asleep, Jonathan looked something like a tic tac toe board, his arms and legs flung out horizontally, and an arm each from Crayton and Jim lying vertically along his sides, pinning him down.

"I wouldn't know about that. I just work here," Howard answered flatly. One thing about Howard, he's never gotten in trouble for telling too many jokes.

"I thought maybe he'd said something about tonight when he gave you the shoes."

"He left the shoes, as usual, in the kitchen. You probably tripped over them before breakfast."

"Probably. I was thinking about something else."

"Like?"

"Like what time dinner would be."

"Ask Momma."

"Now you know Pop's not going to tell Momma what time he's going out. He'll just show up in the kitchen and ask for dinner."

No reply from Howard. I tried again.

"So I thought maybe you'd know. Maybe Pop let it drop to you."

"Nope." Howard had wrapped an old polish rag around his hand and buffed Pop's shoe with it so fast that the leather warmed up and started to glow. He barely knew I was in the room.

I sighed deeply, a cue that got me no more attention from Howard than Tinker's tears got her. I would have to get some help from Momma.

In the kitchen, on her enameled metal table, the kind that goes rusty in the cracks from the sea air's limp kiss, Momma was pushing around a hunk of bread dough with her peculiar hands.

As a young woman, just come to America from Ireland, Momma

worked in a laundry back East and her job was to feed the large items, like table cloths, into a presser. The presser had two heated rollers inside a heavy metal sleeve. A worker could pull down the sleeve around the rollers by pressing a button on the left side of the machine.

When the sleeve pulled down, the two rollers turned in on themselves so that any item, like the edge of a tablecloth, would be drawn in between them. The rollers would pull the tablecloth in, flattening it with heat and force, and would roll it out on the other side, ready to fold.

Momma's job was to keep the tablecloth feeding in smoothly so it would exit the rollers wrinkle free. Her hands were constantly tending to the cloth, stretching it tight just before it rolled into the machine. Wrinkled cloths had to be redone, and since Momma was paid by the finished tablecloth, mistakes cost her time—and money.

One day, the laundry got a load of wash from the Cardiffs, a Welsh family of coal miners who had come to the United States as a clan. They had worked and saved for each other, and had bought the whole mine. They now lived in a castle-like home with an interior, their maids told anyone of Momma's crowd who was listening, that defied description.

"There's more polished wood, linen and hand sewn lace than any Cardinal has seen in a lifetime," exclaimed Lizzie O'Carty, the maid's helper who sat next to Momma at church each Sunday. "The only thing that house is missing is an altar."

The tablecloths from the Cardiffs were wider than any Momma had ever handled and were embossed with graceful lilies framed by softly curving leaves. As she fed them between the steaming rollers, her fingers moved steadily up and down the run of the roller, eliminating any bunching of the fabric.

But the cloth was too wide to control, and it began to angle in between the rollers so that the left edge of the cloth headed toward the right and the right edge started to slip out of the rollers. Momma leaned over to her right to try to push the cloth back in the roller, but kept her left hand feeding in the left edge of the embossed linen beauty. Without looking at her left hand, Momma could feel folds beginning to form under it as the table covering started to run into the machine askew. She pushed her fingers under the folds and shoved desperately towards the rollers, hoping the cloth would be pulled tight and flat by the rollers. Under the folded, gentle linen, Momma's fingers were shielded from the heat of the rollers until too late, until the tips of her four left digits felt the pull of the rollers that crushed the flesh and bone into the rich weave of the lilies.

It happened so fast that at first there was no pain. Helplessly pinning her in place the hold was absolute and the outcome was clear to Momma. Her fingers were gone. The woman on the next machine lunged at the off button, but the machine had resolutely done its job. There was no insurance, no pain killers but whiskey, and Momma had to pay for the ruined linen cloth, but she never complained. Momma wasn't one for pity or even introspection. Whenever she would tell us the story she would include just one sour commentary: despite her paying for the bloodstained tablecloth, she wasn't allowed to take it home. The owner of the laundry claimed it as his.

Now there was a smooth ridge along her knuckles where her four fingers were amputated. Her thumb, which had to do the work of all five appendages, loomed hugely muscular over the rest of her hand. She kneaded the bread into a seamless mass.

The kitchen window was open and the gauzy curtains played on the breeze. The smell of the bread floated freely, and mixed with the fresh leaf and buds-a-burstin' scent of June. Somewhere for someone life was probably wonderful, I thought, but I had a problem to solve.

Tinker sat at Momma's ankles. She rubbed the smooth surface of Momma's cotton stocking with one hand. Sighing, she fed herself with the other whatever crumbs she happened upon. Jonathan sat up at the table practicing for his future job as head teller at the San Juan County bank. He was dividing the excess flour into small hills, smoothed and skimmed into the exact same size. Momma would reach for more flour to incorporate into her dough, and Jonathan would yelp when she flattened a flour peak.

Jonathan and Tinker looked up hopefully at me when I came in. Occasionally, just very occasionally, I bounced them on my knee or launched them into the air for a free fall ride back into my arms. They started to whine, hoping for such an occasion.

Momma, too, looked at me with purpose in her eyes. I had to think fast and sidestep their incipient plans.

"You know," I began, with my most sincerely thoughtful look, "it would be nice to build a real swing for these two ruffians."

"Tinker's still a little small. She can't hold on yet," returned Momma. Her draft call was taking form.

"That's what I was thinking," I fibbed. "But then I thought, let's make a swinging chair. You know, something with sides, and...and armrests!" I beamed helpfully.

"Now, that would be something to see," said Momma.

Jonathan looked at me suspiciously, as if I were a candidate for a loan with very little collateral.

"And me? I don't need no chair."

"Any chair," I countered.

"Howard says 'no chair'," he pelted me back.

"Howard..." I began, but Howard, with Pop's shoes glowing like black diamonds in his hands, finished the sentence as he crossed through the kitchen headed for the backdoor.

"...Howard is so strong he doesn't need stupid grammar rules," my brother added.

"Exactly," I continued. "That's why Howard and I can make two swings. One for a little girl, and one for a big boy, like you Jonathan."

Howard stopped in his tracks and turned toward me.

"Swings?" he looked to Momma for confirmation. Momma shrugged and looked at me.

"Two swings—one like a little chair, to be safe," I raised my eyebrows, questioning his willingness.

"With what wood?" he asked.

"Now there's the problem," I sent out air whistling a little between my teeth, as if defeated.

"Just what I thought." said Howard. "Anyone can have ideas. You gotta be able to do something about the ideas."

"They'll be another day for swings," appeased Momma. "Now, I was wondering about today..."

Before she could go on I waded in.

"You're right, Howard. It's stupid. The wood I have is too heavy."

"What wood?" Howard nearly yelled now.

"Augie, if you're going to do nothing but tease, I have plenty of other work for you," interrupted Momma.

"I'm not teasing," I got a serious, perturbed look in my face.

"I have wood. Good, nice planks. They're just too heavy for me to carry out here."

"Where?" Howard was removing the laces from Pop's shoes, but checking my expression for signs of a joke. Jonathan had gone back to forming flour mounds. He usually ducked away from situations that might disappoint.

"At Miss Paletto's. She says if I clean out her garden and trim her hedges I can have the planks. They're pieces left over from the fence she built."

It wasn't a complete lie. I did have the planks and they had been Miss Paletto's. But they weren't at her house any longer, and they hadn't exactly been earned by doing chores.

"And besides," I continued to engage a surprised Howard, "the tree's too high for us to hang a swing. We couldn't."

"Speak for yourself," Howard grunted. He turned, left the laceless shoes on the shelf by the door, and started outside to wash the laces in the outdoor sink. From the doorway he yelled back, "You bring the wood, I can make and hang a swing."

The imaginary picture of Momma's two sweet young children, placidly swinging and humming away their long summer afternoons, wafted back into the kitchen over Howard's shoulder. Momma stopped kneading just a moment, long enough to let me know she could be convinced.

"I'm going to get the wood, Momma," I asserted soberly. "Crayton and Jim are down at the stream. I'll take them with me to Miss Paletto's. We'll bring back the wood."

"Would Crayton be able to help you?" Momma's vision of the swings began to waver.

"Sure..." I faltered. "He'll. ...he'll carry something. Maybe we'll cut it right there," I added weakly.

"Now how can you cut before you measure?" Momma questioned.

"We'll think of something for him, I promise," I said and started to the door before any more of Momma's intuitive foreboding could stop me. "Just get Howard to go borrow Mr. Jackson's hand drill, OK, Momma? And he should get the rope hung from the tree."

"Be back by lunch, Augie. Swings or no swings, understand?"

"I promise."

I flew out the door and to the road. At the bend in the road, out of sight of Howard, I turned towards Mr. Dockton's strawberry farm, not towards Miss Paletto's house in town.

Five

Strawberries

Since we lived on the outside island of the Puget Sound group designated the San Juans, we were lucky enough to have definite windward and leeward sides. Most people lived in the town by the bay at the leeward tip. Land was pretty cheap up on the windward hills where we lived, but farmers like Mr. Dockton preferred the protected land toward the center of the island.

If I had turned westward, on the narrow lane down to the windward coast, I would have found Beacon Beach, a wild place only good for shell collecting and maybe some grazing. Even before we knew of the grisly discovery to come, it was too craggy and forbidding to be my favored retreat.

It had sand ground fine from years of tides and winds, and faces of granite with irregular ledges rose up from the narrowest sandy stretch. It was gusty and desolate, and once, on a dare, I had climbed down from the jutting cliffs above to a ledge that was said to lead to a pirate's cave.

The place was known as Shore Heights and my fingers were stiff and raw for hours afterward from grabbing on to rocks and straw grass in the sharp cold. My hands lost their grip on the last tuft of grass and I landed with a thump on the ledge. I peered into the cave and got a good nostril-full of raccoon urine and rotting birds. I hollered up to Carl Anders to lean over and witness my success, then I pushed myself back up the hillside, digging in my boot toes and my fingers to any dirt wedged between rocks that I could find.

I collected on the dare—Carl stood at the top of the granite head with two fly fishing lures he unceremoniously handed over—and I'd never been back since.

Instead of Beacon Beach, I reached the edge of Mr. Dockton's property and vaulted the wood fence. Mr. Dockton had shielded his strawberry crop from hungry eyes with rows of corn that were pushing stalks straight up from the ground.

I trotted around the corn and ahead of me, in the green and red-dotted strawberry fields, I saw figures bent over under straw-boaters that anticipated the noonday sun. Men in threadbare cotton undershirts and dusty sweat that settled into the creases of their arms and shoulders reached or bent to the work. Jim's shock of thick black hair wasn't evident. Maybe Doc Strawberry, as local farmers called Mr. Dockton, had tossed them off his land, their history too fresh and fiery to forget.

In the first row of strawberries, Gravelly Boston was picking the ripe fruit and tossing it into the basket that hung from his shoulder. I never knew Gravelly's real name, only that he was one of the more forthright Irishmen that came west from the Boston ghetto. He would show up at Sunday mass, clap the men on the back and shadowbox with the boys. He said he liked picking fruit the least of all the jobs he knew, but in the Depression, he said, there's not enough of the torture of work to go around. He complained in his deep, gruff voice more than most of the migrant workers. And if Gravelly had gotten Mr. Roosevelt's ear, the President would have listened up.

"Looking for your crazy brothers?" Gravelly's beefy face turned to me, his mouth serious but his eyes amused.

"I suppose they're not doing any harm, but I hope Mrs. Mohan hasn't spent their profits yet. Crazier than drunk rabbits, them two." Gravelly looked over a few rows and with a bob of his head indicated my brothers' work area. A few other men, none of whom I recognized, chuckled.

"They're working rows we already worked," one yelled over at me. "We call them the 'backward brothers.'"

I swore to myself that if I found even one rivulet of juice on either of their chins, I'd turn and walk straight home. They'd be on their own explaining themselves to Pop.

I strode across the three intervening rows to find Jim and Crayton in postures of disrepair. Down the dirt lane, between strawberry plants, wooden baskets were scattered on the ground. To the left, under the plants, Crayton was lying on his back. Closer to me, Jim was on all fours and, as he crawled backward toward me, he dragged a piece of carton with him. It looked like a game of choo-choo train that two three-year olds might make up.

My Irish temper turned my ears red and made my eyes go hard and unseeing. I took two huge steps toward them, my fists in balls of rage. The toe of my shoe caught the edge of a basket and strawberries bounded out of the overturned container. I stopped short and looked down the row that stretched ahead of us. Six full baskets of ripe berries lay in the dirt between the rows.

"Watch out, Augie, you'll crush them!" Jim had come up from the flat carton to a kneeling position to call out to me. Abashed, I quickly bent to put the berries back into their holder.

"What...how...are these all yours?" I stuttered now, but the blood was receding from my earlobes.

"It's working fine," Crayton called out. "But go get some more baskets. We're running out."

I simply stood there, staring.

"You know Crayton has no joints," said Jim. "He slithers along underneath the plants on his back and can see all the low strawberries everybody else missed. He just knocks 'em onto this old flat box and every once in a while we come to a wooden basket, I dump the strawberries in and we keep going."

"I've got a lot of bugs down my back and I sure would like a drink of water, but other than that, things are fine," Crayton crowed.

"At this rate, Augie, we'll be home before Pop even wakes up!" Jim added.

They were right. While the other workers were stooped in back breaking angles over the short plants, Jim and Crayton had scooted down a long row filling baskets from plants others had given up for empty.

I tripped over myself running to Mr. Dockton's water pump, where a bucket and tin cup were available. The bucket caught the cool water as I forced it from the ground, and the tin cup scooped the drink from the bucket into Crayton's deserving mouth. Refreshed, he and Jim kept up their systematic collection of strawberries, while I collected the already filled baskets, and brought them to Mr. Dockton for weighing.

In between shunting their baskets to the scales, I filled a few baskets on my own. Before the worst of the heat and lunch time hunger could end our enthusiasm, Crayton, Jim and I were lined up to receive from Mr. Dockton exactly the three dollars and twenty-five cents we needed.

Doc Strawberry pursed his lips hard when he counted out the money, and I thought he might be thinking he should hold back some, maybe as some kind of reminder that in the past we had been more trouble than today we had been help.

He extended his hand with the bills and coins that amounted to our pay, and then pulled it back. Jim and I did a quick intake of air that made a gasping hiccup, a sound less manly than I liked to admit. Crayton stood quietly, looking at Doc calmly.

"How's your father these days?" Doc asked.

"Sends his respects," Crayton shot back before I could answer. "He's just fine."

"You don't say," said a dubious Doc. "I've seen him around town, but haven't had word with him since..." Doc hesitated and scratched the back of his head, then continued. "Since last summer, you know."

"He saw us off this morning and said 'Promise me you'll do a good job now, boys', and we said 'Sure, Pop, it's a promise. And, well, we just hope you think we did keep our promise, Mr. Dockton." Crayton smiled pacifically up at Doc Strawberry, who looked as though the sun had set in the east.

"Well, my, my, a man can never be too sure of things, can he?" Doc smiled, took hold of my hand and dropped the money into my palm.

"You sure did keep that promise. Thanks, boys. There's an extra quarter in there for some ice cream. And give my regards to your father."

Without a word to each other but as if on cue, the three of us turned and sprinted towards the road home.

Six

A Wooden Swing

The money was like a handful of magic and Crayton carried it buttoned in the back pocket of his knickers because he and Jim mostly earned it, and anybody in San Juan County knew not to give Jim anything that oughtn't to be lost. As logical and collected as he was, he was also famously absent-minded.

We ran, we trotted, we walked in hops and skips, in long strides and then we ran again. On the way I explained to them how and why I planned to calm Momma's and Howard's suspicions. I told them everything but where the wood was really stored.

"Pretty clever," Crayton complimented me. He kept his hand over his pocket to keep the gleeful jingling to a minimum.

"Pretty tricky," Jim said after a long thought.

"It's only a white lie," I countered. "And everyone will be happy—especially Momma."

"The good outweighs the bad, I suppose," Jim said, barely convinced.

"By about a thousand tons!" answered Crayton. Jim's stride just got longer.

We cut through the woods east of our house and wound up at the edge of town. Crayton managed the walk with an agility I'd never seen before. All the excitement made him forget to fall. The boys lunged through the high grass and onto the town baseball field before I could call them back.

"No farther," I yelled.

Jim stopped short, Crayton ran into his back, and in the short, soft clover filled grass, he sat down involuntarily.

"What is it?" he sputtered.

"We can't all go and get the wood," I explained. "Someone's sure to notice and word will get to Pop. Get back in the woods and I'll bring it here."

"So what if someone sees us? The two of us lurking in the woods. That'll cause talk," said Crayton.

"It's your wood. You have a right to it. You earned it," said Jim. "Didn't you?"

"Of course. But you know Pop. He's so proud. If he hears it took the three of us to cart it away, he'll say some of it was a gift," I argued.

"That's unlikely 'cause..."

I cut Jim's argument short because there was no room for debate. I had to go alone.

"Trust me, I know," I intoned severely.

"You're going to handle that wood by yourself?" Jim asked.

"I can scare up an old wheelbarrow from Miss Paletto."

I shooed them back into the woods and pointed out a large tree stump for their comfort as they waited. Jim pulled a book from his belted waist and began to read out loud to the disgruntled Crayton.

I walked out towards the playing field and when I saw I was out of their sight, I doubled back to the edge of the woods, scooted along until I saw the swamp path, and then turned back into the woods myself.

There must have been some kind of natural spring in that portion of the woods because it was wet all year round. The land was soaked and moss grew up the sides of the trees. The branches and leaves hung heavy and thick, making it dark and cool just as I imagined a tomb would be. No birds chirped, but there was an occasional whispering of the leaves. Once I told Jim it was the sound of snakes slithering, and I half believed it myself. Jim, and most kids I knew, only talked about going down the swamp path.

Once in a while one boy would dare another to go in and catch a frog, but no one could think of a reward great enough to motivate any such dare-deviling, and the swamp path was left pretty much to the deer and me.

I only used it as a last resort—for hiding items that no one could know about. When you share a room with four brothers, no possession is protected, and not even seniority gives special status. But in the swamp, I had found personal, private storage space to be rented by conquering my own fear. I didn't consider it a great deal but my choices were very few. If Momma found out, or if Pop knew, how I had gained such wood, the consequences would be severe.

Down the path about the distance of half the softball field, on a bed of rocks I had collected, Miss Paletto's clear cedar planks lay under branches and dead leaves. Trees crowded in, and a little gully ran along the side of the path, its bank carving close to my woodpile. Down the bank, at the bottom of the gully, I had left my old wheelbarrow. I picked it out of the garbage behind the marine supply warehouse. It had only taken a month or so to scare up a new wheel and now it rolled along like a fine delivery wagon. It needed new paint, but that could come some other day.

Length by irregular length, I loaded down my wheelbarrow. Bending over the last piece of wood, I felt a cold tickle on my right calf. Moss and weeds from the overgrown green carpet crept up my leg, I thought, itching and irritating me. Then the moss seemed to squirm and slither. It struck me like a heaven-sent revelation that a muscular, meat-starved snake was preparing to squeeze my limbs bloodless and paralyze me.

My left shoulder pulled back, my head jerked away, and I shook my right leg with an excess of fury that sent my shoe sailing down into the gully. I swiveled, put my socked foot up against the tree, and beat my leg with a chopping motion of both my hands, hoping to crush the head of the vicious serpent. The smoothness of my sock made my foot slide down to the base of the tree, so I grabbed onto the wheelbarrow for support, and pulled it over on its side, planks and all. Half the load tumbled back down the gully to where the wheelbarrow had been and where my shoe was soaking in a muddy puddle. Exasperated, I sat heavily and yanked up my pant leg, resigned to seeing the horrible damage the snake had inflicted. Right below my knee, a flattened gray slug clung harmlessly to the pummeled calf.

I sat, flummoxed and silly, my innards still trembling and my joints in a liquefied state. If I had not wanted to return to my brothers feeling as capable as when I left them, I would have left the planks to shelter worms and headed home as quickly as my shaking ankles would take me.

But what weak, stuttering explanation would I give to Crayton and Jim? No, the thing to do was to move fast and forget my embarrassing panic. Slipping to the bottom of the gully, I grabbed the planks and dragged them back up to the wheelbarrow. They seemed to avoid my nervous fingers, and I sweated in the cool air. I was sure that boys older than I were in the shadows, watching, laughing, and waiting for more of my shenanigans.

Finally, stumbling, tumbling and tripping, I rushed the haphazardly loaded wheelbarrow up the path. I thought I would stop to rearrange the planks on the field, but even there my desire to leave indignity behind kept me pushing the load along and back into the woods where I had left Crayton and Jim. We could reload the wood together for easier traveling, I planned. Head down and panting, I trundled my load back within sight of my brothers, and I saw, however, that they had their own set of difficulties.

Crayton stood with his knickers down. His loose soft skin had what looked like moving measles. Jim had stripped off his shirt and was beating Crayton with it. I dropped the wheelbarrow down in a hurry and once again it toppled to the side. The planks splayed across the ground but I didn't look back. I ran toward Crayton and saw the measles were milling red ants. They were busily making sense of their new landscape, a process that apparently included biting and stinging the fresh territory. Crayton was yipping like a little terrier, all the while jumping from one foot to another.

Jim's book was left on the ground and I scooped it up to use in the battle against the miniature red army. I started brushing ants off Crayton's back with the spine of the book.

"Not the book!" exclaimed Jim. "Use your shirt, use his pants, but not the book!"

He stopped waving his shirt at Crayton and lifted the book from my fingers.

"But it's his skin," I objected.

"It's my book!" he said.

Jim took the book and placed it quickly but carefully in the hollow of the tree trunk. He swiveled back to his job as ant sweeper. I took off my shirt to use as an ant brush also.

Soon Crayton's odd dance subsided. We had removed and stomped to death most of his red enemies. They lay exhausted and beaten, intrepid pioneers whose only crime was to have explored a virgin land and have marked it as their own.

"I can't move," whispered Crayton.

His thighs and behind were puffing out, his skin mottling white with red, his pores open and stretched.

Tender areas around his armpits and the nape of his neck suffered, too. His face was streaked with tears but not bitten.

"We've got to get you home," I said.

"I can't walk," Crayton reiterated. He seemed more embarrassed than hurt, although I knew by looking at his wincing face his skin was stinging.

"You'll ride on the wheelbarrow," I said.

"Wheelbarrow?" Crayton said.

"Yes, I borrowed it for today," I fibbed.

"I'll push," said Jim.

Crayton watched as we reloaded the wheelbarrow with the larger pieces making a broad bed for him. I could swing over my shoulder the only two planks that didn't fit.

We headed back into the woods as Jim explained what had happened. He had been reading while they waited for me, and Crayton got distracted tracing a rodent trail in the dirt. He squatted and then sat in the dirt to count the toe prints of whatever wood creature it was. He felt the first bite on his groin, but the massing monsters had already climbed past his waist and on to his back.

"I forgot, I forgot about those damn ants!" Crayton mourned from his bed of wood.

"Aaah, the man has a temper!" Jim winked at me.

"You'd better calm down that language or we'll never get you in the door and past Momma," I said.

"Pop says 'damn' all the time," Crayton commented.

"And he gambles," said Jim. "Are you going to start gambling?"

"And he drinks," I added. "Are you going to start downing whiskey?

"If it's wrong for us, it's wrong for everyone," sniffed Crayton.

"Pop pays the bills," Jim and I replied in unplanned unison. We had been well schooled in the paths of authority.

We bumped through the brush and woods to the cutoff back to our house at a brisk pace. Jim's broad shoulders provided the same strength under pressure I would always admire him for. If coolness of mind could be bottled, Jim would be a national industry.

When we arrived home, Crayton was puffier still but he had

gathered his resolve. He rolled off the wheelbarrow without betraying his great discomfort. It was good timing because Howard ran directly to us to see the planks.

"Let's see these boards," Howard said as he lifted one, ran a thumb down its edge, and eyed it for bowing.

It must have been a pretty straight board because he looked at us with some measure of respect. Crayton managed a grim smile in reply. I winked at Jim, and as Howard started to move the wood towards the tree where the swing would hang, Jim ushered Crayton towards the house.

As we planned, I ran to Momma and diverted her attention. She was hanging the laundry on the line at the side of the house, but she left it to come look at our new treasure. Jonathan and Tinker interrupted their completion of a dandelion chain to see this new marvel.

"What are Jim and Crayton looking for?" asked Momma. "Howard has all the tools outside. I hope they know it's a little late for lunch." She turned to give me a meaningful look.

"Crayton cut his knee and Jim's going to put some iodine on it," I answered, meshing my words together to try to act nonchalant.

Jim had actually agreed to find the baking soda and make a paste for the acres of bites on Crayton's rear, legs and torso. The amount of lying I was doing to cover up all the tracks in this adventure was nearing the monumental. But if Momma knew that Crayton had been sitting in the woods long enough to sustain an ant attack she might ask questions that would lead to the whole story coming out.

As it was, we had taken plenty long enough to retrieve the wood, had missed lunch, and would have to do a lot of explaining to get anything to eat before dinner.

"I'm sorry, Momma," I added. "Everything took longer than I thought."

"I worry, and I do not like worrying needlessly," said Momma.

"But the wood's good, don't you think?" I tried to give her a reason for forgiving me. She nodded in agreement. I was safe for now.

Head down, I got busy with Howard cutting and measuring while Jonathan inched closer. He usually steered clear of hammering and sawing, but the prospect of a new toy made him bolder. Howard had a folded sheet of paper jammed into his back pocket that he would pull out and consult every few minutes. By the looks of it, he had spent considerable time planning the form and proportions of the new swings.

Momma smiled when I handed Jonathan the jar of nails to hold. They were nails that Howard had salvaged from old boards and posts wherever he encountered them, and then painstakingly hammered back into a straight line.

"Hand me one every time I ask," I instructed him. He looked doubtful but threw his shoulders back anyway.

"Just one?" he double-checked.

"Just one," I answered.

"No, give him three and drop the rest," grunted Howard.

"Don't be gruff with your brother. He's trying," Momma warned Howard.

"What took you so long?" Howard tackled me instead of answering Momma.

Another lie scooted off my tongue before I could stop it.

"Miss Paletto asked us to do some extra chores while we were there," I said, keeping my eyes on the nail heads I was hammering.

"Well, very nice of you three to take the time," Momma said. "You must be hungry."

"A little," I smiled warmly at Jonathan. "Nail, please."

"Got it," crowed Jonathan.

"Some stew for lunch reheated?" Momma asked.

"Good enough for me, thanks," I nodded.

Howard coughed.

"You've eaten already," Momma said to Howard.

"I know, but I'm working awfully hard, too." Howard worked the saw against the wood rhythmically. He looked like a bean pole with an anvil grafted on its shoulders.

"How about a bowl of gravy with bread for you?" Momma answered.

"I'll take it," Howard said.

Momma took Tinker by the hand and led her towards the house.

Jonathan stood a long moment, his loyalties torn, but then quietly put the nail jar on the ground and headed in behind Momma.

Howard had made several good, clean cuts. A few more nails and the swing would have a shape. I stood back to see the wood's swirled grain take the form of a seat and then watched as Howard nailed together the pieces for the chair swing. He had cut the board in progressively narrower pieces so that the back of Tinker's swing had a look of crafted design and made our concoction look less primitive. Howard talked about what he could do if he only had some real carpenter's tools.

"I'd curve these arm rests here to fit their elbows a bit better, that's for sure," he sighed. "Put a little rounding there on the seat under their knees. There's lots more that could be done on this one."

I didn't see any problem with what he was making as it was, but it's a wasteful proposition to contradict Howard when he's in a rare good mood, so I just nodded. Besides, Howard and I were going to make all my deceptions become something useful. I was feeling friendly.

"So, I got you an extra bowl of gravy," I started to kid Howard.

"And a bowl of stew," he replied.

"What do you mean? Momma said..."

"You didn't get this wood by doing chores for Miss Paletto," Howard broke in.

"What d'ya think, I chopped down a tree?" I joked.

"Oh, it's Paletto's wood all right, but you didn't sweat a drop for it," he shot back.

He continued with a triumphant smile reminiscent of Pop's cruelest moments.

"That's Bert Harrison's wood. He told me about the good clear cedar he lost to somebody in a dice game. He wouldn't tell me who but I figured it was somebody I knew or he wouldn't have mentioned it. I forgot until I saw it here. It might as well have his initials carved in it." Howard had stopped sawing now and was rubbing his stomach.

"I am so hungry for some stew. You won't really want yours. You'll be too overtired from bringing back the wood, won't you?" He didn't wait for an answer but headed toward the sink to wash up.

I didn't say a word. Howard had me by the tail of my secret. If giving up my stew was the only price to pay to cover up my gambling, I thought, the scales of justice were still tipping my way.

Jim and Crayton had just come out from the house to the yard when Momma came out and called us to the table. After she served us and turned back to the stove, I pushed away from the table, muttered something about being too hot to eat, and passed my bowl over Jim's surprised head to Howard.

"Here, Howard. Make another good swing. I've got to run the wheelbarrow back to Miss Paletto."

"Me, too," seconded Jim, and passed his bowl to Jonathan, who was seated at the table watching us with a thumb in his mouth.

"I don't want another lunch," yelped Jonathan.

"Lord, don't worry, I'll take care of it, little Johnny," said Howard as the screen door bounced shut behind me.

Jim came through in a hurry.

"Wait, I'll go with you," he said quietly.

We stepped off the stoop together, but then I held him back gently by one arm.

"No, stay here, and make sure Howard doesn't get to talking too much when Pop gets up. He keeps talking about how long it took us," I said.

"Pop's already gone to town. Howard told me. And besides, Howard would never put two and two together," laughed Jim.

I wished I could be so sure, but I had much more to hide than Jim. I told Jim to just keep Howard busy.

"Sure," he agreed. "But here, don't forget the strawberry money for Miss Paletto. Crayton didn't want to give it to me, but I guess I can trust you," Jim smiled.

With my concerns for covering all my untruths, I had forgotten the real reason for the strawberries, the wood, the wheelbarrow, the ant bites and the swing. I took the money and put it in my back pocket.

"And Augie, see if you can bring back some calamine lotion. Crayton's in a bad way," Jim said.

"And with what money?" I asked.

"Use the extra quarter," Jim urged.

"Fine, I'll tell the pharmacist that Tinker got bit," I answered. "He'll give me a little extra."

After all the fibbing and inventing I'd done so far, what did a little more matter?

Seven

Lime Cakes

The next day the swings were built and hung from the tree. Howard had worked pats of lard into the rough twine rope so as to cut down on friction as it rubbed against the tree and against the soft palms of Tinker and Jonathan. He had knotted the loops of rope against the branch of the tree just right so that it swung easily but did not twist out of control. The Go Ahead Boy was in fine form, aware only of his handiwork.

The work of the red ants, however, needled Clayton to a restless misery. He had barely slept and had to disguise his discomfort at breakfast by clenching his hands in his lap so they would not wander about his formless middle scratching the white-hot bumps of erupted skin. There was not enough calamine lotion in all the San Juan Islands to stop the itch. Jim and I played cards with him until it was time to leave for church.

We walked to St. Ann's, a stone and timber building near town. There, Father O'Hare led the Irish parish, with a sprinkling of Polish and Italian families, in a brisk but reverent Mass each Sunday. On Sunday, the girls wore their best clothing, and brushed their hair twice as long. I know because of Sarah's preparations, but also because of how the girls would glow in the church candlelight. Jim and I often discussed our favorites, although we were careful not to be overly impressed. Being impressed might lead to being smitten, being smitten could mean being in love, and love was not what we considered a natural state.

Jonathan and Sarah walked hand in hand down the lane, an alliance of convenience on both their parts. If she walked with Jonathan and answered his detailed questions about the world of work as she knew it in the cannery, Sarah would not have to answer Momma's questions about Mason Burke.

Then Jonathan, for his part, did not have to trail behind Howard, Jim and me, bathing himself in dust and incomprehensible chatter about sports, nor did he sacrifice his dignity clenched to the hand of Crayton, who represented to Jonathan one of God's miscalculations. Crayton's inability to define his own waist injured Jonathan's sense of balance and proportion. Momma carried Tinker in her arms.

We got to church at least as happy as when we left home, an experience common to us in the absence of Pop. Pop had slept in as always, and since he had left for town the day before well ahead of the planks arriving, we still hadn't told him about how the swings had come to be. Momma had only told him that we were planning to build something. I used the thick fog of Father O'Hare's sermon to plan my strategy.

"Pop," I'd say. "Pop, look at how happy Tinker and Jonathan are out in those swings." No. Why would he want them happy? No, it would be better to disavow any happiness. "Pop, we worked an awful lot just to produce two worthless little swings. What a nuisance." No, he'd see through that and think we were proud of them, maybe attached to them somehow. "Pop, can you believe Jonathan is happy on that ugly old thing we made?" No, now we're back to somebody's happiness. "Pop, Momma said we can't nail steps on to the tree now to make it easier to climb because the swings are hanging there." That's good. Let him think Momma is ruining something for us and all he has to do is back her up. Nobody has anything special and Pop won't find any fun in tormenting us. When I mention the steps to Mom of course she'll nix the idea and I won't be telling a lie. I just need to keep Jonathan from giggling with delight as he did the evening before when he felt the breeze in his face as he swung like a pendulum on his new seat.

We filed out of church and spent ten minutes or so looking at the rabbit's tail that Mike Kelly had bought in Anacortes and discussing with him the length of time it would take a train to go from Port Townsend to San Francisco. Because Crayton listened so much to Jim, he felt himself to be as widely read as any of the older boys in the parish and so he interjected his opinions with a confidence that belied his ten years. Some of the other boys may have wanted to swat him on the back of the head for being so cheeky, but since Jim and I treated him nearly as an equal, and because most of the time his facts held up, they listened to him patiently.

Momma chatted about the town's affairs with other lady parishioners, and finally we headed back to our house in a knotted group with Sarah trailing slowly behind, thinking, no doubt, of Mason Burke. The sun was warming up the day.

Pop was waiting for us. I saw him sitting in a wooden folding chair on the grass near the front gate to our house. We all saw him and instinctively our conversations ground to a halt. Sarah was pretty sure that Pop's attitude of quiet ambush had nothing to do with her this time so she breezed by us, through the gate and on up the front steps to the house without so much as provoking a word from her father. Jonathan tried to do the same but Pop caught his hand as if in greeting, but then he gathered Jonathan into his lap while never letting his own eyes stray from my face.

I thought I had prepared the terrain of battle well, so I drew in a breath, pushed open the gate ahead of Howard, Jim and Crayton, and then held it open for Momma and Tinker. Momma set Tinker down on the front walk, but before she could distract Pop with talk of dinner, he spoke to me.

"Some fine-looking wood is hanging from the tree in the back yard, Augie," Pop said. "Why, I figure the leftover scraps are worth more than what you've earned in the past month. Where'd you happen to get that wood?" He spoke, as usual, in dry, clear tones with no hesitation. A barking watchdog showed more humility than Pop.

"It's pretty good wood, it is," I said slowly, trying to find a legal position. "I earned it doing chores at Miss Paletto's."

I wanted to glance over at Howard to see if in his face Pop might be reading a reflection of my lie. I kept from looking at him only by meeting Pop's eyes and holding them.

"She pays in wood now, does she? Got a lumber mill in her back yard that nobody knows about?"

Pop's gaze never left me, but at the same time he lifted up Jonathan and placed him on his knee. Jonathan stared at me with high concern, as if one false move from me might result in his being dismembered.

"She had it left over from some fixing up she was doing. A porch she was putting on, I think." I answered as casually as I could, pacing my words to Pop's, wanting to match his nerve with mine.

"Miss Paletto is building a porch of clear cedar. Now that is news. I'd say maybe the Friday Harbor City Council is paying its librarians a mite too much these days." Pop looked at me with the delight of a veteran pitcher who had just hurled a fastball past the nose of a rookie outfielder.

Why I said Miss Paletto was building a porch I'll never know. The nervousness I felt trying to hoodwink Pop made me think that a lie should be a whole lie, with no part that was true, so I changed Miss

Paletto's fence project to a porch. And by the time I started fabricating explanations for Pop, even I wasn't sure what the whole truth was.

Momma glanced at me quickly and I saw the alarm in her eyes as she envisioned this sunny Sunday turning sour. My plan to create a distraction by mentioning nailing the steps onto the tree trunk was useless. I resorted to the timeworn ploy of deprecating humor.

"She doesn't know, Pop. She's just a woman. Why, she had the whole porch painted over. She probably doesn't know the grades of wood," I assured everyone with an easy smile. Pop did not smile back.

"So you took planks of expensive wood from an honest woman, knowing you were taking more than your due, knowing you were deceiving her," Pop looked steely-eyed at me.

"She was going to burn it, Pop. She wanted me to cut it up for firewood. I just offered her a deal. Instead of money, I took the wood." My argument was good, I thought, but it bothered me to fall back on the defensive, as if I were cowering somehow.

"You got more than you earned," Pop declared with a cold disgust in his voice. "The swings are not yours. No son of mine will take any charity. That's what the woman was doing, performing a charitable act, and you—so anxious to have, to take—you couldn't even see through it."

Jonathan had gone rigid on Pop's lap when he heard the death knell ringing for his precious swing. He knew enough not to cry but the effort of containing his disappointment made his chin stick out and his eyes moisten. Momma saw his emotions brewing up so she took his hand to lead him into the kitchen. To help him get down from his lap, Pop gave Jonathan a cuff in the shoulder blade, as if to knock some tiresome pet back to the ground where it belonged.

"Well, if the woman wanted to freely give Augie something, Edward, I don't see a problem," Momma said, bending down to steady Jonathan before he could cry out. This intervention was the development I wanted most to avoid. Momma might step into a conflict with Pop without knowing the whole truth.

I still had the option to tell the truth, but admitting that the wood did not come directly from Miss Paletto but had been won in a dice game against Bert Harrison, who had actually been given it by his father, who installed Miss Paletto's clear cedar fence, might end up implicating Crayton and Jim. My mind raced over the problem of admitting evildoing myself while hiding the fact that yesterday morning our time was not consumed at Miss Paletto's but rather in the forbidden strawberry fields of Mr. Dockton.

But before I could find my voice to start the wary process of threading the truth through a needle of deceit, Howard spoke up. He had been leaning against the gate watching the standoff with studied indifference, but aware, no doubt, that I was in a tight corner.

"It's a good idea, Pop," he said, looking meanly at Jonathan.

Slouching with his hands in his pockets, Jim stood between Howard and me. At Howard's words, Jim's hands balled into fists fattening his pockets. His head jerked toward Howard and his blue eyes blazed.

"Why, now, what are you ..." Jim started to turn on Howard, and Crayton, standing behind Jim, put his hands out as if to grab Jim and hold him back. Howard was undeterred.

"Don't be fools," Howard said harshly, and took a step toward Pop. He turned his head back towards Jim, Crayton and me, but much to our surprise, instead of narrowing his eyes in one of his usual expressions of disdain, he winked.

"It's a dirty deal and you know it," Howard said disgustedly, turning back to Pop. "We leave those swings up and pretty soon we'll have the rest of the town holding a pity party for us. I'm burning them today," he continued.

Howard rolled up the sleeves on his shirt to reveal his arms, his muscles already bulging above and below his elbow. Crayton understood the message and chimed in.

"A bonfire! This'll be great! We can gather enough brush to get this thing going hot," Crayton crowed.

Jonathan's complexion turned ash gray when he heard the chorus of pyromaniacal enthusiasm. Tears welled up in his eyes and he buried his face in Momma's dress when even Jim put in that maybe a good fire would be some fun.

"Pop, help me," Howard stood over Pop, in the stance of a challenge but uttering words of manly companionship. "Let's make twigs of those swings. You and me with a couple of hammers and those things'll be unrecognizable. They'll burn up in a lickety split. Help me get them down."

The sun had come over the trees at the side of the yard, and Pop's slim frame rested lightly on the spare wooden chair. He squinted up into Howard's face, which was full and flushed, with a wide mouth and square, white teeth. His shirt had wrinkled in the heat and his underarms were stained with perspiration.

"You boys are capable of undoing what you did all by yourselves," Pop said coolly, but he drew back enough just enough to reveal his regret at having unleashed the combustible urges of his wildest son.

"We shouldn't have an untended fire," Momma said quietly. "Remember."

"I," said Pop, rising from his chair by pushing it back away from Howard, "said nothing of a fire." He smoothed out his vest and righted his cuffs with a tug.

"I said they are not Augie's. He will earn them by doing extra chores. I will have a list of the necessary chores in his hands before dinner. When the chores are done, I will pay Miss Paletto the money Augie has earned with his chores."

Pop looked at Momma and smiled with satisfaction. Momma took Jonathan's hand, and not looking back at us, went up the steps ahead of Pop and into the house. Pop followed but stopped at the door and turned back to us for one last shot.

"You boys needn't help Augie. He took the wood. He can earn it." With another smile, he followed his wife into the house.

When the bodies of the young Chinese lovers washed ashore they were, as I said, clasping one another. They were also tied to each other, her right thigh bound to his left thigh. If even Chinamen were no strangers to love, why had my father been denied this capacity?

I turned to Howard and clapped him on the back. "Fast thinking," I said.

"You better figure this out. I don't want nobody touching those swings. They are measured and sawed just right," Howard answered.

"Figure what out?" asked Jim.

"The wood didn't come from Miss Paletto. When Pop goes to pay her, the whole story will come out," answered Crayton.

"How do you know about the wood?" I turned to ask Crayton.

"Well, I figure that Pop is right, it was too much for Miss Paletto to pay you for some measly chores, and I know Miss Paletto is smart enough to know not to paint over clear cedar, so I figure you must be lying," Crayton explained. He sat heaped on Pop's wooden chair, and looked glumly at Jim.

"You lied?" Jim barely breathed out the question to me. "To Momma, too?"

"I'll do the chores. I'm getting my punishment," I mumbled back to Jim.

"Well, get ready because they'll be worse where that came from," intoned Crayton.

I flashed a warning glance at Crayton, but it was too late. Howard took a step back.

"What else?" He deepened his voice. "What else are you hiding?"

"We worked at Mr. Dockton's yesterday. We got enough money to pay Miss Paletto to bind up our pages into a book," blurted Jim.

"Oh, jiminy," Howard sighed and pushed Crayton off the chair so he could sit down on it. Crayton barely noticed. He was scratching now.

"All this for a book," Howard said, amazed. "And the swings? Why make the swings?"

"A distraction," I answered. "A sort of red herring."

"Well, you got yourself a red herring that looks more like a two-ton whale," commented Howard.

We laughed. We forgot our Sunday clothes and lay out on the grass and laughed. We laughed like little boys at the circus who only want the show to keep on going and never stop. I loved having my brothers beside me. I loved knowing that we each knew what the other was up against. We told Howard about the money Jim and Crayton's book might win and he was duly impressed by the prospect of a one-hundred-dollar prize.

"With your prize money, you can buy me some tools. I've contributed quite a bit to this project," laughed Howard.

"Sure, no problem. That'll keep you busy while Jim and I are off working on our next book," answered Crayton, rolling over on his side and propping up his head in his hand.

"We might be let out of school so we can lecture at the library in Anacortes," Jim added. We looked at him, abashed by the fact that he was completely serious.

"Really," he continued, "it's no joke to be published by a university. It could be a beginning of something. A career."

"You're not going to run off and buy yourself a hat anytime soon, now are you?" asked Howard.

"After the third book," answered Crayton. "And I'll have a suit with long pants."

The thought of Crayton in clothes that resembled anything but knickers and a cap sent us rolling about on the grass again, the laughter shaking us down to our toes. Jim was the first to stand up and brush himself off.

"It's a grand idea," I said, getting up and clapping him on the back.

With a smile and gentle nod he said, "We'll see," and we all walked into the house to eat.

Pop presented a long list of jobs right before we sat down for midday dinner, and he announced he would be home all afternoon, so I started working at about one o'clock. Pop sat in the back yard and watched as I cut firewood, weeded, cleaned the outhouse, buried the garbage and scraped paint off the windowsills that needed re-painting. My brothers knew to disperse and I worked on, thinking about the colossal joke this punishment would become once Crayton and Jim's book were published and awarded the university's first prize. I thought about how the family would admire my ability to solve problems and lead my brothers when they were stymied. Even Pop, I thought, would allow that his eldest son had a head on his shoulders and could be trusted to see an advantage and work towards it.

Without an audience, Pop tired of his role as supervisor. At five o'clock he announced he needed to visit a friend in town, and he directed me, in no uncertain terms, to finish all the jobs he had enumerated in a complete and diligent fashion. He set off, dressed in his light summer suit that showed some wear at the elbows, a white shirt slightly frayed at the cuffs, and his straw hat. Impeccably shaved, barbered somewhat less perfectly by Momma, and crisply pressed, he could have been going to a New York theater or a government job. Instead, he traveled on foot to a town of clapboard storefronts where men stranded in the midst of a

Depression looked at each other in disbelief and suspended understanding.

At six o'clock, Momma called me to the kitchen. She had fresh lime cakes set out on the table. They were one of her few culinary successes: round, firm and spread with sugar frosting with bits of lime peel in it. Usually, she made them only for birthdays. "Eat," Momma said. Tinker and Jonathan sat at the table with me, friendlier than two traveling salesmen.

We ate, the bitter-tasting lime outweighed by the sweet combination of sugar, flour, butter and egg. Then, outside I pushed Tinker and Jonathan on their new swings.

Eight

It's Better to be Honest than to Tell the Truth

Pop walked into Friday Harbor that Sunday afternoon to see about a job. If a man needed to hustle himself some employment, and the man made his money from the sea, he would naturally go to the port and see what he could garner.

A port town is usually a bustling place where there is no dearth of stories and storytellers. So a businessman from another town might arrive and want to meet some customers. To make friends and to make himself likeable, the businessman tells some stories to the hotel clerk, or the restaurant waiter. Maybe some stories, usually about people in the town, get traded back. Some names come up and some introductions are made. The businessman meets more people and eventually some new customers. I've been living a long time now and a lot of things have changed. Planes, rockets, computers, lasers, surgery without scalpels and factories without live workers have come down the road while I've been watching. But port towns still work the same way.

That's not to say that the bustling of a port town operates on an even keel. The pace can slow and the number of stories can decrease, so that people latch on to any story that comes along and tell it again and again until the rhythm of the town picks up. During the Depression, Friday Harbor had its share of long, slow days with the same faces telling the same tales, or worse, not bothering to talk at all. Lack of money made some people more resourceful, and made a few people more grateful for what they had. But it made a lot more people flinty and severe, doubly wary of the easy laugh.

When Pop went to town that Sunday afternoon, I figured he would hear some stories, but nothing that pertained to Miss Paletto, the wood or me, because to look for work he didn't go to places where he'd hear light-hearted stories about boys doing chores for librarians.

I don't mean to say that he liked to be hard and mean. Like many other people, Pop went where business was conducted, and if business was conducted by mean or unfriendly people, Pop could hardly stop to protest. Pop had seven children, and like us or not, he understood he had to feed us.

It's just that Pop didn't bother to seek out the other kind of people, to find a balance, to see if the world could be pictured in more than one way. He heard the mean stories and he accepted them as the way to talk about the world. Maybe I would be the same way if Momma had left me early. It's not fair to criticize a man who lost out so young, but I dearly wished he had become better acquainted with kindness.

Nevertheless, Pop did feed us, and that day he went to find ships that needed a navigator like him. At the hardware and marine supply store in town, sailors and their captains would gather to play cards and drink gin. To most people, gambling was like germs: an undesirable element of human interaction that should be contained whenever possible. On Sundays, to avoid the attention of the more religious folks, the men entered through the back door of the warehouse. But, if anything Sunday was a busier day than any other, and Pop knew his best chance for needed cash would be Conawalski's.

Mr. Conawalski wasn't afraid of work. I'd always expected him to work well into old age, stocking the shelves and showing customers the various block and tackle combinations he could offer them. He was the kind of calm and practical man who could deal with setbacks.

Once, as the story goes, Mr. Conawalski was retrieving a rudder handle from high up on a wall of shelves. Wally, as most adults in town called him, set his wheeled ladder at the base of the shelves and climbed up to the box he needed. Unfortunately, he had not placed the ladder accurately, and he had to reach for the box he wanted. So he put his right foot on the shelf and reached out with his right hand. In reaching, however, he pushed away with his left foot, and the ladder moved to the left, leaving Wally clutching onto the narrow shelves.

Unfortunately, the customer who had expressed interest in the rudder handle had by then moved to the back of the store to examine the quality of boat lines on hand. He didn't notice Wally's predicament. While he waited for either the customer to return to the shelf area, or a new customer to walk through the door, Wally took inventory of the number and kinds of rudders and handles on the shelf, and when the customer finally rescued Wally by holding the ladder steady under his feet, Wally descended to his work area behind the counter and made a note of the number of items he needed to order.

As it turned out, the customer owned a fleet of fishing boats and was so impressed with Wally's calm that he ordered all manner of rudders, lines, nets and hardware, and widened Wally's already admirable profit margin. Wally was considered a quiet, unassuming man who was nobody's fool.

Mrs. Conawalski was a worried, anxious woman with fluttering hands whose projects were as relentlessly energetic as they were changeable. I knew of her from Momma's conversations about the St. Ann's Ladies Group and because Mrs. Conawalski, who was as Polish as her husband, stood out from us, the mainly Irish parishioners at St. Ann's. Father O'Hare was the only person I knew to be indifferent to nationalities, probably because he had enough work containing the energies, sinful and otherwise, of his flock to worry about their backgrounds.

Mrs. Conawalski had, at various times, started a clothing bank for the poor of our county, a collection to commission a statue of George Washington to stand at the head of the main pier in town, a club to make quilts for South American babies, a petition to stop the sale of cigarettes to minors, a committee to improve the library, and an association of birdwatchers.

She spoke continually of the future, of the importance of progress, of what the island needed to improve, and of what could happen if we all worked together. Father O'Hare said he appreciated Mrs. Conawalski's suggestions and, in fact, he implemented programs that she had begun but later abandoned for unknown reasons. He regularly appointed her committee chairwoman or lay deacon and often featured her social exhortations in the parish bulletin, although one spring afternoon when I was helping him weed the church garden, I saw him wince when Mrs. Conawalski slipped through the gate and surprised us both, crouched in the dirt, with her high-pitched greeting.

From my point of view, Mr. and Mrs. Conawalski were a smiling couple that had mysteriously produced three children wholly unlike them. None of their three daughters, whom my brothers and I knew from school and church, ever expressed an inclination to better anyone or anything in the town, but rather gave the distinct impression that they were already better—and that we would be better if we didn't forget that fact. Jim, Howard and I kept our distance from the Conawalski girls, and I wondered at times, if families could ever be known from the outside.

At any rate, Mr. Conawalski was allowed enough free time from Mrs. Conawalski's industrious planning so that on Sunday afternoons he could open up the back of the warehouse to card players, both local and outsiders. He had a sort of soiree without the tea and fine language. That Sunday, Pop showed up, contributed his share to the pot for gin, and settled into playing poker and asking who might be needing a navigator soon.

That day wore on into evening, Pop uncharacteristically lost quite a few hands, and still no one who needed Pop's services rotated into the game. Fishing was good, perhaps too good, because prices were down and profits were slim. Many of the sailors and boat owners in the game reported that boats were forced to cut back on crew and captains were required to do the work of the navigator also. Towards the end of the evening, when Pop had folded and was sitting in the corner finishing his last drink, Wally opened the door to admit Petesy Corrigan, one of his few close pals.

Petesy was a tall, graceful man, close enough to forty to have a little stiffness in his back but still so young looking that a glance from him could make women blush. Petesy glanced because he was single, but women glanced back who were not.

Despite years of hard work that allowed him to buy his own fishing trawler, the *Carolina*, Petesy had no wealth to speak of. Once at the store I had heard him say that his memories were his bank account, and when I got home I asked Momma what he meant. All she said was that if I had enough time to think about Mr. Corrigan I certainly had enough time to do chores and she sent me outside to cut firewood.

Petesy usually wore handsome knit sweaters over a well-cut pair of wool trousers, was clean-shaven and had thick, brushed red hair. His face was symmetrical with a strong chin, and when he smiled large white teeth flashed pure charm.

Charm was the word most often used in conjunction with Petesy, but Petesy himself told me that charm could be a dangerous thing. It happened once when Mr. Conawalski was letting me root around in the back of his warehouse for a wheel for my wheelbarrow, and Petesy was sitting at the card table addressing a set of envelopes, each with a note and a bank check, to be mailed out while he was away fishing. Petesy told me that he was writing to women he had once charmed or they had charmed him, he wasn't exactly sure.

I asked if they were having a birthday or something special like that, and he laughed, looking over at me with wonderment. Then with a grin, he said that actually there was a birthday involved and that when I was older I should take care to only fall in love once, and not once a year like he did.

"Not that it matters," Petesy murmured. "Women'll get you comin' and goin'."

Charm, I also learned, was the kind of virtue that tends to spread itself thinly, like a veneer, over a person's life, and doesn't penetrate deeply like honesty or loyalty. Petesy would smile at ladies, more kindly at babies, and even at young beanpoles like me. But according to Pop, he cheated at cards, treated his crew like dirt, lied about his profits, failed to take care of his boat, and skunked out of paying honest wages to anyone he could, even if they were fellow Irish Catholics.

As luck would have it, Petesy walked in to Conawalski's that Sunday looking for a navigator. Petesy smiled at Pop and clapped him on the back. He wanted to go out the next Wednesday for a four-day run up a little north of Vancouver Island. They said later it seemed like Pop suddenly wasn't interested in work. He looked away while Petesy stood with his overgrown grin over Pop's shoulder. Finally, Pop grunted his assent, and without bidding the group goodbye, stomped out into the back alley and headed home.

The next morning, Pop was up early, saying he couldn't sleep. As we five older children downed our milk and oatmeal, he sat morosely at the table. He had a cup of Momma's coffee gripped at the handle, and while it etched its acid signature into his stomach lining, he stared furiously.

I sucked in my breath and tried my best to ingest breakfast with the bare minimum of accompanying oxygen and no superfluous movement. My brothers and sisters followed suit and breakfast finished without a spoon clicking against a bowl, or a chair scraping the floor. We excused ourselves with the faintest of comments and averted eyes. We learned to eschew sympathy and to cultivate disciplined diffidence as though our lives depended on it. They probably did because that day Pop seemed to hate every detail of his life, hate every tie that bound him to his wife and her pack of children and all the responsibilities that made him— a bright and able man, deserving of every freedom great capability should bring—beholden to Petesy.

As I slipped into our sleeping porch to get my cap and work gloves, I quietly rejoiced that Pop would be gone for a few days. He was too agitated and bellicose to ever convince of anything. Though he hated lowering himself to work with Petesy, at least it would be enough time, I hoped, for him to forget about the wood planks and the swings, and for me to somehow get things settled with Miss Paletto before he stumbled onto the truth about my dealings, or non-dealings, with her.

We were all in the kitchen, parading stiffly past Momma in order to receive our sack lunches, when Howard, who was the last in line but the least able of us to efface himself, reflexively asked Momma for the largest possible apple she could find for his lunch. Pop's attention alighted menacingly upon him. Out in the yard, Sarah, Jim, Crayton and I watched and listened through the screen door as Pop addressed Howard.

"Stop me if I'm wrong, son, but aren't you one of seven?" Pop's hard smile stretched tight across his narrow, handsome face.

"Any apple will do you for," Momma said while she hastily gathered the rest of Howard's provisions. She was sending him and Crayton off for a morning of wild loganberry picking, and she would have liked to see them out the door before any unpleasantness could unfold.

"No, no, Kate," continued Pop. "If the boy thinks he deserves more than the others, let's let him explain himself."

Momma had one hand on Howard's back and nearly had him out the back door and on towards his food-gathering mission. But Howard, never the best practitioner of convenient indifference, turned to answer.

"It's no problem. I can find another apple on my way. I don't need a big or a small apple."

Pop sprang to his feet, pulled Howard back from the door and out of Momma's protective shadow. He wheeled him around and grabbed him by the collar of his dusty flannel shirt, pulling his wide, freckled face close to his own angry snarl.

"You don't need a thing, do you," he growled, the spit forming at the corners of his mouth. "You just need your Momma to cook, and clean, and sew and wash. You just need your Pop to work his fingers out in the cold and the wind so you can have your hot stew and your apples. You don't need a thing. You just need everything."

Pop pushed Howard toward the door at the same time he yanked free the pull-string cloth bag containing his lunch.

"Go. Get. Don't come back until dinner time. You go find some nice big apples. It'll be easy. You don't need anything." Pop walked the bag over and set it on the sink, then he walked back to the table, wiped his mouth with a napkin, and laughed quietly, as if at a small, gentle joke. He waited until Howard, red-faced and stumbling, headed out the kitchen door for a long day of hunger that no amount of apples or loganberries would appease, to turn to Momma.

"Well," he said and cleared his throat. "I have some preparations to attend to here and in town. Don't prepare any lunch for me."

We watched as Howard, his eyes in their anger unseeing and out of focus, miss the last step, go down heavily over his bent leg, then straighten up. His arms rotated over his head as if he were swimming to the surface from a deep dive. He hurtled by us toward the path to the woods followed by a wordless Crayton. We all thought it best to be quickly on our way.

Once we were down the road a few paces and around the first bend, Crayton scrambled out of the woods and hailed us.

"He doesn't want any part of it now, but I know he'll be hungry later," Crayton puffed.

We knew that Crayton was right, that for Howard, food would always conquer pride, and that Crayton would end up paying the price for Pop's pointless discipline. Sarah, Jim and I broke our butter sandwiches into pieces, and we each gave Crayton a third to crush into the pockets of his knickers to share later with the becalmed Howard. Crayton loped back to the woods with a wave and his signature laugh.

Jim and I trundled down the road behind Sarah, who was now forced to keep up a brisk pace to make it to the cannery in time. She had to be at her post by the rinsing sinks before the whistle sounded.

Jim and I had it easier. We worked at the dock as cleanup boys and as long as we hustled when we unloaded boats, our punctuality could be more casual than Sarah's. We were paid by each boat captain according to our speed and efficiency. If we decided to take a break, eat our lunch—or often in Jim's case, read a book—no one rebuked us. There were plenty of boys to take our place, load crates onto wheeled carts, roll barrels to waiting trucks, push a broom, and collect the coins a captain offered.

Jim would lay out on sunny afternoons, often stretching his lunch hour into two on the wooden fishing pier at the end of the dock, away from the noise of the boats, reading the biographies of great men or Greek mythology or some novel by Hardy. He ate whatever Momma had given him, if he ate at all. You could tell where Jim was reading because gulls would circle overhead, waiting for him to leave open his lunch sack as he fell deeper and deeper into the thrall of his book.

I loved the tales he would tell me on the way home of gods and god-like men, but rather than read them myself, I took my lunch hour at the Harbor Cafe. Mr. O'Neill was the owner and as sloppy as the water splashing over the dock at his door, so he fed me soup and brisket for lunch, and I washed the dishes and scrubbed down his counters in payment. I'd wrap up the food that was left over from my plate and in the late afternoon, when Jim and I needed another lift, we shared the leftovers. It's funny the way things even out. Jim took care of our entertainment and I took care of our stomachs. By five-thirty, the boats that were coming in were in and unloaded, and we walked back home.

That Monday, we had worked our day as usual, and as we headed away from the dock and towards the road to home, we saw Miss Paletto walking towards us. Mondays the library was closed and it was not odd to see her around town doing her errands. There was a trace of doubt in her walk, however, and she looked thoughtful, as though she had more to say than words to say it with. I stopped in my tracks, but Jim's step quickened and his smile widened. He approached Miss Paletto with the happy question on his lips.

"When will our book be ready do you think, Miss Paletto?" Jim almost shouted.

"It's ready," she answered, but without a smile.

"I can't believe it!" Jim said and whirled to look at me with a heady joy in his face. "Where is it? Let's go see it, please!"

"Well," Miss Paletto began in tones more measured than usual, "it's on the way to your house."

Jim blinked a few times and looked questioningly at Miss Paletto. "How's that? Did you mail it?"

"How was it ready so soon, Miss Paletto?" I asked. "I calculated a good two weeks or so before you could get it to Seattle, bound and back again."

"I actually had it sent out before you gave me the money. It just seemed more sensible because of the contest deadline. Then my father was coming out here from Seattle to visit on Sunday and I asked him to pick up the book and hand-carry it to me, as a favor. And he complied." This last part she said almost by way of apology, as though her surprising efficiency had caused us some kind of discomfort.

"It's lovely, Jim. Worthy of any library in the state," she smiled at Jim. It was high praise coming from a woman who could quote the classics.

"Could it win the contest?" he asked.

"I'd give it a good chance," she answered.

"Well," said Jim, speechless with pride.

"When could he see it?" I asked. Jim's eyes, glinting in the afternoon sun, locked on Miss Paletto's face. She seemed to feel the intensity and quickly looked instead at me. Instinctively, worry furrowed down my brow.

"When would we be able to get it?" I asked again.

"When your father gives it to you," she said. She tried to smile cheerily, but it turned out to be more of a grimace.

"Pop?" blurted Jim.

"I thought I would walk to your house to deliver it this afternoon, but I ran into your father on the road coming into town. I showed him the book. It is really something to look at. I thought he would be impressed."

"Pop." Jim let out the word like air escaping from a sagging balloon.

"And I guess he wasn't interested," I said, offering Jim the little hope I had left.

"He actually listened very politely as I explained your work, and he started back on his way to town," Miss Paletto said. I smiled and Jim's chin rose back up again.

"He's not really one for books," I said, trying to regain composure.

"Right. The book wasn't really what caught his interest, I don't think," Miss Paletto continued. "He was continuing on toward town but then he stopped and came back. He asked me a question about some planks of wood I supposedly had given you as payment for chores you did, Augie."

"Oh," was all I could manage to respond.

"When I said I hadn't known about any planks, he asked how Jim and Crayton paid for the book, and I said I didn't know for sure," she went on.

"And he took the book?" I asked shakily.

"Yes, he took the book. When I said I didn't know anything about planks or the money, he took the book. I hope I haven't spoiled something for you boys, but I couldn't lie." Miss Paletto looked steadily at us, neither with distaste nor with pity. She looked as I imagined one would look through the bars at suspects awaiting trial. It was a look of suspended judgment.

We left Miss Paletto and headed home with rising anxiety, tripping on our own fears, trotting with an electric current of jitters sparking at each step. Jim barely spoke, but it wasn't anger that kept him from talking to me. I could tell by his face that his thoughts were on one thing and one thing only. He wanted to recover that newly bound book.

About two-thirds of the way home Jim made his sole comment. "If it's all right, I'm donating it to the county Library. I promise." He said it more like a prayer than any communication that needed a human response.

By the time we got to the house we had broken into a run. We both leapt the gate, darted around the side of the house, and took the steps up to the back door two at a time. We landed in the kitchen with one long stride and then stopped on a dime. The book was laid out on the kitchen table, stately and serious.

The cover was black and thick. Square cut letters in silver print decorated both the front and the binding. I saw the words *James and Crayton Mohan* in print so bold it seemed embossed. Our family name was on a book. Our family name could be handed from reader to reader. Our family name could bring science and learning to people who had less. We knew things. We were a family with something to offer the wider world. I was so proud of my brothers I wanted to hoot and dance.

Jim went to the table without a word and reached out a finger to touch the black weave of the cover. If I wanted to dance, he must have wanted to sing from the roof. A sharp cough from the hallway door made him look up. Pop stood smirking at the door. He had a pale, tear-streaked Crayton by the hand.

"The author is home. The other author, I should say. It apparently took two of you geniuses to cook up this scheme." Pop had the look of fury temporarily contained by disdain.

"It's a book," said Jim. To Jim, that fact would explain everything and forgive anything. Pop seemed to take it like salt on a wound.

"Do you think I can't see? Or maybe I can't read? That I'm some dumb fisherman that doesn't know what a book is? That doesn't know what's a trick and what's a lie?" The fury was beginning to seep out of Pop and into the room.

"Where's Momma?" I asked dumbly.

Pop turned toward me, jerking Crayton with him. "Your Momma can't help you now. You can't stand behind her, little sneak," he sneered. "Your name is not on the book, but I know you're in this, too."

"Pop, it's just a book," I said. "There's nothing wrong with a book."

Pop slapped away Crayton's hand, leaving him to sway unsteadily and then lean against the door jamb. Pop seemed to want to give the full force of his attention to Jim and me. I wanted to slip away, out the door, and make Pop chase me. Out of doors, in the summer afternoon, fleeing down the road, I might have a chance to run the anger out of him. Maybe in the warm afternoon's slanting rays, the light would temper him, make him see the worthlessness of all this meanness. I didn't move, though. I knew Pop would never chase me but only sit and wait for me to return.

Pop's eyes narrowed and his lips curled out the furious words. "How did you pay for this book? And don't tell me about some made-up chores. I spoke to Miss Paletto and she knows nothing about any chores, any planks, or how you got the money for this book."

I didn't respond but it didn't matter. Pop was on a tear and someone would pay. The scent of the whiskey on his breath had reached me. Pop gestured accusingly at Crayton. "Your poor idiot brother here doesn't know. Just doesn't know a thing."

Crayton tried to speak but only sobbed instead. I took a step towards Pop to try to get between him and Jim and the book.

'You stole the planks, and then you stole the money for the book. That's how you work. You've been turning over your money from your dock work to your mother, she told me so." Pop looked me in the eyes. "So there's only one other explanation."

He waited a long moment and then bared his teeth. "You're a thief and I'm going to see to it you get your punishment."

Face to face with him, I no longer felt like the sober one. I felt reckless, as if hurtling downhill on a bicycle. What mattered now to a son whose own father hated him?

"I didn't steal," I spoke rapidly. "I won the planks playing dice."

There, it was out. The truth that had fueled all my lies. I had been gaming, betting, gambling—call it what you will. I hadn't wanted to tell my brothers because it was a portion of my life that set me apart from my family, a part that belonged to only me and made me a man on my own. I could win and lose in my own world, and what I won belonged only to me. I had done all I could to avoid telling Pop because he furiously objected to any of his children participating in any kind of gambling, but his adamant stand came from his particular experiences. My life, I felt, was my life to live. I was due my own experiences.

Now Jim would be hurt, and Momma would be outraged, but if I tell the whole truth, I should say I still didn't fully regret the facts. At some point, I thought, I had to grow up and have my own life, and my own vices.

There was no reason, however, to involve the others in this new unburdening of my secrets. I decided once I was in hot water I might as well take all the blame. Maybe, I reasoned, it would come at a wholesale cost.

"And I got the money for the book picking strawberries," I continued, looking at Pop. "Mr. Dockton let me. It only took a couple of hours. I told Crayton and Jim where the planks were hidden and while I was picking strawberries they went and got the planks."

"Mr. Dockton!" Pop's voice was raspy. He took a step back from me and hardened his gaze. "You went and did business with that man? A man I expressly told you not to talk to, let alone to go begging to?"

"I'm sorry. I needed the money. It seemed like a good idea," I finished somewhat lamely.

Pop's eyes were nearly bulging from his head. "You're going to get a beating you'll never forget. You're going to wish you never were born," he shouted.

"It's a lie!" The sound thundered out into the kitchen. I looked around for Howard, thinking he had barged in to set things straight. But

Howard wasn't there. The words had come from Jim, now holding his book in his lap.

"It's a lie!" he repeated. "I worked with Augie. We both picked strawberries. He did it just to help with the book. Then we got the planks to make the swings just to confuse everyone about where we'd been. We didn't hurt anyone or anything. But we did it together."

For a moment, no one spoke. Pop looked around the room as if he had suddenly lost interest in the topic of books, lying, stealing, underage gambling and consorting with the enemy. He walked toward the sink and paused to look back at us. Then he lifted the metal washbasin up and out, turned and set it on the kitchen table.

"Give me the book," he said to Jim. Jim didn't move.

"Give me the book," he said again. Jim was barely breathing.

"Pop" I said as I walked toward him and he slapped me across the face.

He went to Jim and took the book off his lap. He opened it and grinned.

"So nice. Such nice work," he chuckled.

He dropped the book in the washbasin, took the matches off the shelf by the sink, struck one and held it to the side of the book. The pages, lying flat and smooth between the two covers, caught on fire immediately. Jim laid his arms on the table and buried his head in them. Crayton sunk to the floor. I was still holding my cheek, pain and anger setting my face on fire. I grabbed for the washbasin but Pop pushed me away with a deep bark.

When the fire had consumed the pages it petered out, not hot enough to burn into the heavy book covers. Pop took the wash basin to the back door and tossed it out, like so much garbage.

"So you're not thieves, but liars. Well, that's what liars get. It's out there, sitting in the dirt outside. Two pieces of burnt cardboard with liars' names on them. Go ahead, go clean it up. And I don't want to see any of you before I leave on Wednesday. Don't come out of your room while I'm around."

We obeyed him. We didn't see him again before he left to go on Petesy's *Carolina*.

Nine

The Sea is not Your Friend

The first Chinese man I ever saw got off a boat I was unloading at the dock a year or so before Pop went off to Vancouver Island with Petesy and before the bodies came ashore at Beacon Beach. This man had a starched white collar and a black suit and his shoes were normal lace-up black leather. Surprisingly, he carried a Bible and when he spoke to me he called me "brother." He asked me where he could get a meal and I showed him the Harbor Cafe. Mr. O'Neill told me later, to my shock and surprise, that the man ate with a knife and fork.

Some Japanese folks lived on San Juan Island, mostly working the farms and speaking English, but Jim told me that China was different from Japan. China, he said, was a very large place where people ate peculiar food, like chicken feet, and pretty much didn't care for God.

I spent some time wondering about that man. He looked different to me even in his American clothes, but then, he must have seemed different to his own family, too. What could make a man leave his own kind only to come to another place and live as a misfit? I concluded that China must be an awful place full of unhappy people if he were willing to choose such a lonely life.

It was not wholly surprising to me, then, when I heard about the bodies at Beacon Beach. It was Saturday afternoon, three days after Pop had left on the *Carolina* and five days after the burning of Jim and Crayton's book. No ships were unloading and I had finished cleaning Mr. O'Neill's kitchen, so I sat warming my face leaned up in the front of the cafe against the signboard advertising *Hot Stew*.

Ammie Kilgore ran towards me like a boy on fire. I could hear his footfalls on the wooden planks of the dock that were suspended over the rocky beachhead that served as our town port. I squeezed closed one eye in order to squint open the other. When I saw Ammie, the barber's son and one of Howard's huskier baseball teammates, come charging down the dock, I opened both eyes wide and scrambled to my feet.

"Augie, where's Howard?" he panted when he came to a halt a foot or two past me. A tackle from that boy felt like the unwelcome separation of your skeleton from your organs, and I was glad to have been spared it by stepping out of his path at the last moment.

"Momma's working at the church today so he's watching Tinker," I answered. "What's your interest?"

"My interest is gonna be your all interest," Ammie, born Ambrose Faustus Kilgore some thirteen years before, sputtered out at me.

"My Pa got a call from the sheriff that they found some bodies up there at Beacon Beach. He's going to fetch them because they need some real fixin' up after being drowned. Wanna ride up and see?" Ammie asked, pretty full, as usual, of the fact that his father had a business central to the healthy functioning of our island economy, and therefore, owned a truck. He operated a mortuary as a side business out of some rooms behind his barbershop. Despite the Depression, there still wasn't enough dying on the island to warrant a full-time funeral parlor.

"I guess," I answered slowly, trying to hide my great revulsion and even more enormous interest at the thought of seeing some gnawed on bodies close up.

"You're scared," laughed Ammie. "Doesn't matter about them. They're Chinese bodies. It won't bother you," he assured me knowingly.

If we were as much a mystery to the Chinese, as they were to us, I imagine their isolation as the most foreign of immigrants must have been just about complete. I knew their language was indecipherable because some Chinese candies, individually-wrapped in a thin, waxy paper that seemed more appropriate for medicine, trickled into the bins at the grocery store every once in a while. The markings on the wrappers made me think that the Chinese were laughing at us with these spider-like symbols that could not possibly carry any meaning. I imagined them cooking up pots of monkey or rattail soup in their dark apartments surrounded by statues of false idols and sticks of nose-burning incense.

Pop had told us that plenty of Chinese had gathered in one area in San Francisco, so many that people called it Chinatown. He said the area made the Irish ghettos in Pittsburgh and New York look posh because the Chinese packed children, parents, grandparents, and great-grandparents into the same small two-room apartments. But more than anything, Pop said, Chinatown was full of men alone, men who had left their world and all their people behind, in order to earn a few dollars in our world. However, said Pop, if he were allowed to pick his crew to go up to Alaska, he would pick all Chinese because they know their numbers and work harder than most.

"People try to say they shouldn't be here, but I don't. I believe it when they say they built the railroads because I've seen them work and you have to give them credit. They worked the cannery here on San Juan until they got thrown out. They survive on soup and they don't stop until the job's done. Never seen anything like it," he told me once. Since Pop didn't often have words of praise for anyone, let alone a whole group of people, his comments stuck with me.

I trotted behind Ammie down the dock, almost forgetting about Jim. When a gull screamed, I looked back and saw Jim on the pier with his nose in a book and several birds inching their way towards his bag of crackers. I whistled loud and sharp and he looked up. But he came only slowly, even when he saw my motioning him to catch up with us.

Jim's pace was a message to me that he was not one whit happier with me than he had been for the past five days. Finally, he, Ammie, and I hopped into the bed of Mr. Kilgore's truck for the ride out to Beacon Beach, and Ammie told Jim and me everything he knew about the bodies.

Jim listened, terribly quiet the whole while. God forgive me, but I was hoping that the excitement of seeing dead bodies up close would shake Jim alive. For five days, he had barely spoken and had eaten even less. I had apologized ten times, and would have gone on to an eleventh if I thought it would bring some life to his eyes. Crayton cried most of Tuesday, and on Wednesday he and I buried the remains of the book under the swings so that we would always remember where it was.

But Jim only lay under the covers in our room, unwilling to answer our questions and pleas. Thursday morning he had gotten dressed and followed me to the docks, but when the first boat arrived and the hearty, joking seamen tossed us lines and set to bringing crates down the gangplank, Jim retired to his reading pier, choosing mourning over income. Friday and Saturday had brought the same routine. Soon, I thought, Momma would begin to notice the decline in our earnings, and when the explanation came out she would be mad at me all over again. As it was, no one in the house was sparing me an extra smile.

Ammie was unimpressed by Jim's silence and kept on talking the whole trip out to Beacon Beach. Mr. Kilgore had a large leather kit of tools riding in the back of the truck with us and Ammie opened it up to show us the technical horrors of his father's work as a sometimes undertaker. Even large towns in those days often relied on barbers or furniture makers to do the work of cleaning up corpses when there was no trained mortician. So it was no surprise that our little island used midwives for birthing and a barber for burying, and occasionally in between one might run into what they called a teacher. Otherwise, everyone was their own professional in the business of living.

The kit had tubes, forceps, scalpel, scissors, pins, buttons, eye cups, a razor, a comb, and a handheld suctioning pump. There were small flasks of liquids that Ammie said his Pop used to clean out a dead person's veins. A large hypodermic needle to inject that liquid was strapped inside the bag. There was a pair of thick rubber gloves and even lipstick and rouges he used to pretty up lady corpses. At the bottom of the bag lay several old washrags, laundered but still stained from work with previous corpses.

I handled some of the tools out of the kit with reluctance. The thought of a body being shaved, injected, and cleaned out and the body giving no sign of a response made me shudder inside. Mr. Kilgore might as well be working on a wax figure. For this forlorn person, all hope was gone for a change, for a future or for a chance at any laughter. He would just be working on a fleshy casing, on something that bore a resemblance to a human but was now closer to dirt than to life. The tools were for working on a container, once valuable, that had become nearly worthless.

Jim kept his distance from the tool kit but didn't take his eyes off Ammie as he told the stories of things he had heard and seen working with his Pop in their business. People go rigid, he told us, and the skin doesn't so much turn white as it goes cloudy gray like the sky before an ugly storm.

"I want to see what Chinese skin does," said Ammie. "This'll be something new."

"Are you gonna touch them?" I asked, betraying my discomfort.

"Touch 'em?" laughed Ammie. "We're riding back with them."

Jim and I exchanged glances briefly and Ammie had himself a good chuckle.

"What did ya think? They'd ride sitting up with Pa in the cab?" He looked at us with derision, which I calculated, was the whole point of his inviting us along on this excursion.

We rode a bit longer, listening to Ammie's tales, but then the tires stopped bouncing along dirt and gravel and hit the sandy ground of the beach. We jumped out of the bed to keep the truck from miring in the sand, but we followed it across the beach to the hard, wet surface of the shoreline where Sheriff Murphy's own car stood.

These were the only vehicles on the beach, but the beach was populated nonetheless. Clutches of boys and men stood talking. Some were dressed in their street clothes and held on to their bicycles; others were in heavy boots and carried the hoes they had been using for clamming. Some younger boys carried baskets of clams, and held on to their fathers' jacket hems while staring over at Sheriff Murphy. Clearly the littler ones understood that this was a momentous occasion, but not much else. Any girls who happened on to the beach were quickly shooed off by the men and sent home. On one side of the beach, however, the sand turned to rock and then climbed straight up in a tangle of rock, bushes and dirt. At the top, on a flat promontory, a few women and girls had gathered to watch the morbid scene from a safe distance.

There was a quality to the air at Beacon Beach during the summer that I have never sensed anywhere else since, and to this day, it has been bound up with my memory of those corpses. The air would come up in the summer from the sand, steamy and warm, with the acrid smells of salt and seaweed. The salt gave our skin a stinging dryness. There was a breeze usually, but the steamy blanket of air kept it at bay and it was only a whisper above our heads or out over the waves. It was as if the mild weather could not penetrate the persistent harshness of the rocky shore.

As we approached Sheriff Murphy, we saw the tarp on the beach that covered a long, narrow mound. Mr. Kilgore and the sheriff kneeled at one side of the tarp, and Ammie, Jim and I gathered on the other side, crouched down and listening intently. Even Jim was caught up in the sudden rush of life one feels at the side of death.

"I thought you said two bodies, Sheriff?" Mr. Kilgore asked, looking at the single bump in the sand.

"You'll see." The sheriff moved toward the cover on the sand. Before he touched the tarp, he looked gravely at us. "You boys here to help?" We nodded stiffly in reply. Then he bent over and lifted the tarp cautiously off the sand.

Wet, black hair was what I saw first, and then some clothes that were ripped and twisted. Gradually, I saw that they lay front to front; bound at the waist, but any romance was gone from their faces, which were scraped and swollen. Their eye sockets were empty, bloodless holes. Their feet looked as though they had exploded, and bone and stringy cartilage showed through at their ankles. The Sheriff must have arranged their clothes back on their bodies as best he could for modesty's sake, but still through the gaps the remaining scraps left I could see the gashes and black and blue skin. By the curve of the buttock facing me, I also knew that it was the body of a woman, and as the Sheriff pointed out to Mr. Kilgore, the other was a body of a man. They were small and slim; their backs arched inward, their arms around each other.

"Well, now, who would have done this?" sighed the sheriff. He was graying and kind, the son of the previous sheriff, and although he didn't know it at the time, the grandfather of the next sheriff. He hoped everyone would stay out of trouble, and while he knew that was impossible, he always seemed disappointed when the people of San Juan Island went astray.

"Done what?" harrumphed Mr. Kilgore. "Damn chinks done it themselves."

"I think someone tied them up and threw them off a boat," said the sheriff.

"Sheriff, with all due respect, these bodies are suicides," said Mr. Kilgore. "Look at their wrists," he instructed. Ammie stretched out his hand to touch the woman's arm and Mr. Kilgore slapped it back.

"Don't touch," growled Mr. Kilgore. "These Chinks got a disease like as not."

Ammie's pop had on his rubber gloves, and pulled up the arm of the woman as best he could from the back of the man and showed the sheriff her wrist.

"No marks," said Mr. Kilgore. "It doesn't make sense that these two were bound at the waist by someone, and then not bound at the wrists. It doesn't make sense."

"Maybe so," said Sheriff Murphy. "But what if they were already unconscious or dead when they were thrown overboard?"

Mr. Kilgore pushed hard against the woman's body to separate the two as best he could. He put his hand between the two and pulled out a gloveful of a brown and white cheesy mixture.

"Seems like someone vomited," he said disgustedly. "They were alive when they went in the water."

Jim and I rocked backwards on our haunches, our knees gave way, and we sat heavily on the sand, gulping upwards for sea air. The sun made everything warm and heavy, and I felt nauseated. Jim looked as green as I felt. Thankfully, Ammie paid us no attention, as he himself was growing paler throughout the examination of the bodies.

"And they didn't get thrown out of a boat," continued Mr. Kilgore. "Those feet only got busted up like that because they jumped from some height."

"From where?" asked the sheriff.

"Don't know. Maybe a bridge, maybe those cliffs. Wherever it was, they sure didn't have no parachute, because they hit the water real hard."

In my shock and nausea, I tried to imagine where these two sorry figures could have come from. In my confusion, I imagined them sailing the distance from China, only to be tossed by unexpected waves in the water close to shore. Perhaps, instead, they were up from San Francisco, looking for a lost father who had sailed north to find work. If my parents were scratching for jobs and money, certainly theirs had met the same fate. I longed to hear their story and at the same time I was glad I didn't have to.

Jim stood and walked away from the pathetic corpses, soaked like bony sponges in their salty liquid shroud. He shed his shoes, socks, shirt and pants, walked down to the shore and ran toward the waves. He dove under the first one to reach his thighs. I watched hardly breathing, until his head and shoulders reappeared and he turned to signal me that the water was fine, his thumb and forefinger in a circle. I stripped down to my skivvies and joined him.

"Augie?" he called after I had surfaced a few feet from him. "Those people stink."

"You want to walk home?" I challenged him.

"You're sitting next to them. Not me," he answered.

"Not me. Why should it be me?" I shot back. Now that he had recovered some of his spirit, I had no plans to give up my command as his older brother.

"You lied, Augie. You lied a lot," he said, treading water and squinting into the sun.

"And you told the truth at the wrong time," I responded.

"There is no wrong time for the truth, but there sure is a lot of trouble to be got by lying," Jim answered.

I opened my mouth to continue my own defense but Jim ducked down below a wave, and came up already stroking towards shore. I wanted to tell him that I had meant well, that I had thought I could kill several birds with one lie, but that things had gotten out of hand, no fault of my own. Who could have known, I would have said, that the book and Miss Paletto and Pop and a bottle of whiskey would have all come together at just the wrong moment? Lies, I would have said, are the way the powerless can gain some control.

Jim and I never spoke of the book again. Not until much later, anyway, but that is another story altogether. He and I little by little went back to getting along as brothers, yet I could tell that the authority I felt as the older of the two no longer weighed so heavily in his decisions.

Ten

Take One Look

The bodies were loaded into the truck, with Mr. Kilgore and I doing the work. Ammie supervised diligently and Jim kept his distance.

The sheriff had taken measurements of the corpses and their positions on the beach while Mr. Kilgore complained that people have enough trouble taking care of their own needs and why did they have to clean up some mess made by chinks. They could just wash back out to sea for all he cared, he said, but the sheriff insisted the bodies be taken away and buried.

On the trip back to town the tarp that covered the two young corpses flapped open in the breeze again and again, effectively ruining my sleep for a full week to come. Their hair was dull and knotted, their noses and ears chewed up, their eye sockets gaping, their jaws slack, leaving their mouths round and open as if in irritated objection.

The one fact that mitigated the horror was that there were two of them. Together they had met their end and had gulped down their death. If love had been their object in life, it now joined them forever.

Questions about their love—if it was love that banded them together—occupied my thoughts during the trip back to Kilgore's makeshift morgue. First and foremost, could Chinese love? There are so many of them, I thought, all with the same eyes and hair, the same small bones. There was the problem of their language. It was pronounced as a sing-song, Jim had told me. Could endearing words be pronounced in a sing-song? But there was always the chance, I reasoned, that somewhere in their travels these two might have learned English and could have learned to say "I love you." That accomplishment, I thought, would have put them steps ahead in this romance business.

If they didn't love each other, why did they jump to their death? Perhaps, in their ignorance, they thought one would make the other float, and that together they would form some kind of buoy and they would bob to safety. But safety from what? What was so bad on land that they had to jump? I had enormous difficulty conjuring up anything so terrible that I would be willing to risk my life in an escape.

I sat between Ammie and the corpses. Jim sat at the end of the bed, his arms over the back gate, and his back to the bodies. Jim never looked towards them or us the whole trip. At one point, when the tarp flapped open for one terribly long moment, Ammie squinted hard and then groaned. As much as I resisted giving Ammie any credence, I had to say something about this monstrous mystery that lay near us.

"You're not going to throw up, are you?" I asked.

"No!" Ammie nearly shouted. "I wouldn't lose my lunch over two sick Chinese."

"Sick? They seem more dead than sick."

"All corpses are dead, you idiot. Not all of 'em are sick, too."

Ammie inched even further towards the side of the truck bed, holding on and gulping fresh air as it blew by us.

"How do you know they're sick?" I asked.

"They got the measles," said Ammie. "Pa found the rashes on their stomachs. Both of 'em."

"When were you going to tell me? Before or after I touched them?" I growled.

"You've had the measles. So's Jim. Remember, we showed off our spots to the class that day in school and the teacher put the three of us in the broom closet until the principal could take us home?"

"And the next day Jack Quinn painted red spots on the mop handle and scared Miss Brady half to death when she took it out to clean," I laughed.

"Anyway, Pa says it doesn't help to have people all excited about measles, so don't go blabbing about it. If you do, you'll never get another ride in this truck," Ammie looked at me in that tough way that the untested can muster when they know they're backed by power.

"What difference does it make?" I challenged him, just for the sport of it.

"No difference. Just makes things easier, that's all. They drowned and that's all. It's easier."

I wasn't sure what would make undertaking easier, so I let it drop. Ammie seemed unusually disinterested in sharing his font of knowledge with me.

We pulled up to the rear of Mr. Kilgore's barber shop, and the three of us boys hopped out of the bed faster than bees can sting.

Mr. Kilgore was unconcerned with my fears, and he briskly directed me to help. He and I pulled the tarp and its contents off the truck and carried them in to a metal table in his workroom. Jim called out that he was going back to the dock and he trotted off.

I thought I would make my exit as immediate as possible also, but Mr. Kilgore moved faster than I could and tossed the tarp from the bodies, revealing them fully. I stood gaping at them. They were bloated and disfigured, but none of that ugliness diminished the wonder of their pose. They had held on to each other in sickness and into death, far beyond the formulas that are conventionally set down for constancy. Nowhere in my sixteen years had I seen such an expression of love. Mr. Kilgore heaved a sigh and swore mightily.

"Ammie!" he shouted after a moment's pause.

Ammie tentatively stuck his head through the door grim-faced.

"Pa?" Ammie croaked.

"Check the shed for a pine coffin. I only need one for these two," he said.

Ammie ducked back out and I watched as Mr. Kilgore tried to loosen the couple's clothing.

"Are you going to bury them in something different?" I asked, surprised that I still had a voice.

"Don't know yet," grunted Mr. Kilgore. "For now, I just want to make sure I'm not putting them in a coffin with anything valuable."

He pulled away the collars of their shirts and took scissors to slice the material away from their backs. Across the young man's back ran a thin, tightly braided cord. Mr. Kilgore tugged at it, but it encircled the boy's chest and arms, and so he clipped it with the scissors and pulled. From the front of the body slithered a scapula, still attached to the cord. I recognized it as the kind my mother wore. Scapulas, she said, were not meant to be taken off. I made a gurgled sound of distress when Mr. Kilgore tossed it to the floor.

"I guess we don't have to worry about these two wearing jewelry," he said.

I picked it up to slip it in my pocket and Mr. Kilgore spoke sharply to me.

"Don't touch that stuff."

"I've already had the measles," I answered.

"Oh, so you know. Well, don't make a public announcement, all right? I'm going to load 'em in a coffin, cover 'em with lye, and put 'em in the ground. I'll call Doc Walters, and we'll scrub down the room and that'll be that. You can't take nothing of theirs, or you'll infect somebody for sure. So off you go, and thanks for all your help."

"Is she wearing a scapula?" I asked.

"A what?"

"Another of those necklaces?" I asked.

The Kilgores were Lutherans. Scapulas were created in Rome and used by Catholics to venerate the saints. Usually they had a picture of a saint painted on a square of oil cloth and then sewn on a square of material. Between the picture and the material backing they affixed a relic of the saint: a strand of hair or a thread from their clothing. My own was in a drawer at home, but I knew my mother would not forgive me if I left one behind to be desecrated.

"It's just that my mother would appreciate having one," I fibbed.

"Look, if it turns up I'll save it for you," Mr. Kilgore fibbed back. "I'll save both of them for you."

Ammie opened the door just then, and I took the cue to leave. As I hustled out the door, I heard Ammie telling his father that there were no more of the plain coffins anywhere on their property. A last look over my shoulder told me that Mr. Kilgore was none too pleased. He banged his closed fist against the table and swore again. I let the door close quietly behind me.

I skipped the docks and went straight to St. Ann's to see if Momma was still at work. She and the other Ladies of St. Ann cleaned, laundered and polished for Father once a month. Those donated hours of charity made me think many times that my mother had an overdeveloped capacity for hard work. But many years later, she told me that since the work involved no diapers but plenty of gossip with the other ladies, she considered her days at the church the one holiday no one in the family could deny her.

Momma was in the church sacristy folding linens with her friend, Mrs. Hanahan, when I got there. I poured out the news of the bodies and told my mother about the young Chinese man's scapula.

"They're Catholics!" she exclaimed.

"I don't know. She didn't have one," I answered.

"Well, not every Catholic wears one, now do they?" She raised an eyebrow at me and let her Irish lilt do the accusing.

"I'm keeping mine safe at home. I know where it is," I replied.

"Sure you do. And maybe that girl's is safe somewhere, too," Momma said. "So they'll be needing Last Rites and a funeral."

"They might be needing a lot, but they're not going to get much but a quick burial. They've got the measles," I blurted in my newfound spirit of honesty.

"You mean Mr. Kilgore is burying them without a priest?" asked Mrs. Hanahan.

"That was the impression I got. He wasn't happy at all with having to take care of two diseased Chinese people for a moment longer than he had to."

"That Mr. Kilgore's not happy with anyone who doesn't pray to Martin Luther," Mrs. Hanahan retorted.

"Hush, Irene," cautioned Momma. She was a great believer in shielding children from conflict among the adults. "No use creating problems bigger than the ones we have."

"Did you touch them, Augie?" Momma asked.

"They were wrapped in Mr. Kilgore's tarp. I just picked up their feet and set them down again."

"Well, go wash up and we'll be off. Do more than just wet your hands, now. Soap up to your elbows and scrub."

I did what I was told, came back and Momma folded the altar cloth she had in her hands and slipped it into her bag.

"I'll go to Kilgore's with you, Augie," she said and then turned to Mrs. Hanahan. "If you can, Irene, wait for Father to come back and then tell him where we are. Maybe he can get to Kilgore's before too long."

"Take the holy oil with you, Kate. You never know," said Mrs. Hanahan with a grim look.

Momma placed the small vessel of oil into her bag and we started to walk the half mile back to town at a brisk clip. About half way there Momma sent me ahead at a run to find Jim and tell him to go home to rescue Tinker from the surely impatient hands of Howard, and to fix something for dinner. When I caught up with him at the docks, Jim went home willingly to take care of the little ones.

I got back to Kilgore's as Momma came down the street. She was still wearing her apron and looked odd to me, like a traveling salesman without his case, as she sped down the sidewalk with no child in tow.

Instinctively, I guided Momma down the walk by the side of Kilgore's barbershop to the rear door. I entered without knocking, but I could barely get in the door and Momma was left entirely outside, pressing against my back as if all I needed was some encouragement to make my way inside. But the door knocked into the metal table that still held the two bodies. Mr. Kilgore had apparently shoved the table over to make room for two carpenters' horses on which he now had laid planks of pine. He was about to saw the end off one piece but the noise of our entrance made him look up.

"I'm not interested in an apprentice, Augie. What are you doing back here?" he said roughly, but continuing to work.

"We are here to save these children from a godless burial," shouted Momma, projecting her words over my head and into the fetid-smelling room.

"Oh, now, you haven't brought the family along, have you?" Mr. Kilgore's saw stopped mid-cut. "Don't come in here, Mrs. Mohan. It's no Irish wake and it's no place for a woman."

The bodies indeed looked a good deal worse than even the hour before. They were more discolored and bloated. My distaste must have shown in my eyes since with a disgusted sigh Mr. Kilgore put down his saw and tossed the tarp back over the bodies. He pushed the horses back towards his workbench and pulled the table towards himself, so he could get around it and move toward us. This shifting allowed me to push the door open wider so Momma scooted around me and into the room ahead of me.

"It's a good job you're doing here, Mr. Kilgore," Momma began. "Cleaning up these poor children of God for their burial."

"For the love of Pete," began Mr. Kilgore, restraining his language for the benefit of Momma. "They're two Chinese, sick as dogs and stinking to high heaven. And if that weren't enough, they were either suicides or plain stupid. Brought all of this misfortune upon themselves. If I don't finish this coffin immediately, get them in it, and soak it and them in lye, the good doctor is going to come and close down my shop. Now, what do you want to say before you leave and let me finish the job that the sheriff has dumped on me?"

"They're Catholics, and they need a blessing," Momma pressed on.

"They're Catholics? She's in rags and he's got a pigtail. Who knows what they were doing with each other before it came into their heads to go for a swim."

Momma ignored Mr. Kilgore's vulgarity and continued. "Augie told me of the scapula the boy was wearing. It's of Our Lady of Lourdes. Somewhere he met a priest and learned of Jesus and Mary. No matter what he's done since, you can't take that away from him. He deserves his Last Rites."

"And her?" Mr. Kilgore gestured angrily towards the lumps under the tarp.

"We must assume she entered into grace with him. For our purposes here on earth, she's Catholic, too."

Mr. Kilgore stood with his hands on his hips. He wasn't a tall man, but wider than most and thick muscled. His blondish brown hair mixed with sweat and matted thickly but trimly over his square-cut head. Ammie and Mr. Kilgore shared the same dull eyes and full, meaty mouth that often expressed their disapproval of whatever could not be stacked, counted, or divided up. Unlike my Pop, however, Mr. Kilgore lacked a quick tongue that could serve as a lash. He hesitated in the face of my mother's sincerity, and so lost the battle.

"They're going to God. They'll be talking to God. For all you know, Mr. Kilgore, God has a Chinese translator up there with Him," suggested Momma.

Mr. Kilgore turned his back and headed for his workbench, speaking to us as he worked his way around the metal table. "Bless 'em, then. Do a rain dance, for all I care. But do it fast. I'm going to have vermin in here if I wait much longer."

"We need to wait for Father," my mother intoned.

Mr. Kilgore whirled back upon us. "No, no, none of that. Either you bless 'em or I package them up. All I need is eight nails hammered in and this coffin is finished. Then they're gone."

Momma closed her eyes briefly and bowed her head. For just a moment, she seemed to rock back on her heels. Then she opened her eyes and shifted her bag up towards her so that her good hand could root around for the holy oil she had brought. She produced it from her bag, shifted it to her left hand, and blessed herself with her right. She brought out from the bag a pressed and folded linen cloth, which she laid on my left forearm.

"You're the altar boy now, Augie. Do what I tell you," she instructed.

Momma walked toward the table with a sure but slow step. I was sorry for what Momma would have to see, and afraid of what those horrible faces might do to her. I wished this ritual would end quickly. Later, Momma told me that she was fearful but convinced that no matter what bodily remains she found on that table, the souls that had once been there had really gone to God and were resting comfortably.

Mr. Kilgore folded the tarp back from the blackened, eyeless heads and Momma caught her breath. I saw her shoulders slump a bit and the fingerless hand holding the holy oil dropped precipitously towards the floor. I came up beside Momma and shored up her arm by the elbow. She looked at me, her eyes watered, and a deep exhalation of breath moved her chin and shoulders back up again.

Momma took the stopper out of the vessel of oil. Using her thumb as a stopper, she turned the vessel upside down to spill out some drops. She reached across the body of the boy and made a cross with the oil on the girl's forehead.

"May God forgive you your sins, and lead you to life ever after," Momma prayed.

She repeated the blessing for the boy, put the stopper in the vessel, and turned to me for the cloth. She wiped her hands, and returned the cloth to my forearm. She indicated to me that I bow my head, and together we said an Our Father, and a Hail Mary for their souls.

"Go in grace, and peace be with you," Momma softly admonished them, and pulled the tarp back up to cover their sad remains.

"Thank you, Mr. Kilgore," Momma said before she turned to go. "Father will be disappointed he couldn't get here in time, but we can assure him that what needed to be done got done, thanks to you."

"Well, I'm glad you're satisfied. I'll be finishing the job, then."

"I didn't see any pigtail, though, Mr. Kilgore," Momma said levelly.

Mr. Kilgore squinted hard once at us but otherwise his expression didn't change. "Don't go home in those clothes, Mrs. Mohan. Go some place, change, and burn them. You'll be spreading measles all through St. Ann's parish if you don't," he said and turned unsmiling away from us.

We headed home and met Father O'Hare on the road near St. Ann's. He had fulsome words of praise for Momma's determination to bless the bodies before their burial, and he commended me for my initiative.

"Now, Father, you'll be thinking my boy a candidate for the priesthood to hear you talk," said Momma.

"Worse things have befallen a lad, Mrs. Mohan," he answered.

"I'm not sure he, nor I, could witness more of what we witnessed today and still keep our cogs in balance."

"Did it bother you?" Father asked me.

"It caught me by surprise," was the most I could admit.

"He nearly fainted, and would have, if I hadn't passed him up on the way down to the floor," put in Momma.

"Was there a strong odor, then?" Father queried.

"Saints be listening, I could barely think of them as human beings, Father," Momma exclaimed.

"Then you've been as strong today as any I've seen, Mrs. Mohan. You did a good deed directly for the Lord and he'll bless you."

"I'll take the blessing gratefully, Father, because I imagine Augie will be included, too." Momma glanced sideways at me.

Since the debacle with the book and my admitting to gambling, Momma had kept me at arm's length. Now her evident satisfaction with my efforts, though she tried to dampen it for my benefit, relieved me a great deal.

Father took us to the shed next to his rectory, and went inside the church to the collection bin where he kept clothes and other supplies for the poor. We changed into these other clothes, shoes included, and

Father set fire to our contaminated set right there in the back yard of the rectory. We got home after dusk and just in time to find that Howard had built a bonfire in the back yard, and Jim had set Tinker, Jonathan and Crayton around it to hear ghost stories while Sarah toasted them bread and cheese sandwiches over the fire.

Eleven

Lost and Found

All of us knew that each Sunday morning we would troop off to church with Momma. The Sundays that followed her work with the other Ladies of St. Ann were a special pleasure for Momma and, by extension, for us. The gleaming candelabra and the polished communion rail were her accomplishments, not to mention the white lace trim on the neatly pressed altar cloths. She was light-hearted and smiling, recited silly limericks on the road to church, complimented us on our manners, kissed us after we went to communion, and was generous with the breakfast portions once we were home again. Momma usually baked bread on Sunday afternoons, but those were the Sundays when she would throw in a raisin pie or two for good measure.

After church, Momma stood with the other Ladies in the June sunshine, talking and laughing heartily. Howard had gathered a bunch of his friends around me so that I could recount every detail I could remember of the poor, dead Chinese couple. Crayton had more questions than everyone else combined and I had to promise him I would tell him everything all over again that afternoon to get him to give the others a chance to talk.

Jim joined the group for a while and I was relieved to see him, if not his normal self, at least responding occasionally to the other boys' jibes and jokes with a good-natured pound on their shoulders. He drifted off when the talk of the corpses got detailed. Sarah told me later that Momma had seen her talking a little too long with Mason, and so sent her off with a dime to light a candle for the Chinese couple. Sarah went back into the church to deposit her dime in the metal collections box and found Jim already there, kneeling before the rack of candles set before the statue of the Virgin Mary.

"I didn't pay for a candle," he mumbled to her. "They were just poor Chinese and I don't think Mary minds." Sarah dropped the dime in the box and left Jim's candle to burn on.

When we got home that afternoon Howard and I buried the remains of the fire without being told, and raked the ground over the spot carefully and then scattered some gravel over the area to make it look unused. Pop was due home that evening and while he might not notice a fire ring, if he did, there would be a definite loss in family harmony.

Pop didn't show up by dinner. None of us commented on his absence, but there was no doubt that it was felt. Momma delayed dinner until Jonathan and Tinker were standing forlornly in the kitchen staring at the empty table and sucking on their thumbs.

Howard and I came into the kitchen to wash off the ash and dirt, and Howard reached out and pulled Jonathan's thumb from his mouth.

"For cryin' out loud, how old are you?" Howard snapped.

Jonathan started to cry and Momma came out of the pantry, lifted up Jonathan and set him at his place at the table.

"There now," she said. "Howard's going to set the table and I'll serve the stew when he's done."

Howard and I set the table in what must have been world record time. We ate, more quietly than usual, and several times I caught Momma pulling in her upper lip to chew on it in a worried way. I am ashamed to admit now that at the time I thought how typical it was that Pop could ruin a good day without even being there.

The next morning we got up and went to our jobs despite the feeling of awful stillness in the house. The docks were busy on Mondays so Jim and I kept up with Sarah all the way into town. Sarah's thick hair was wrapped in a bun and her eyes were unusually serious.

"Make sure you boys bring home every last nickel you can today. Pop's not back and Momma's real low. They'll be onion soup for supper so eat what you can at your restaurant, Augie," she warned.

"Where do you suppose he is?" Jim asked.

"I don't much care to know," Sarah said briskly. "But it probably involves wasting Momma's money, so he better show up soon."

We worked hard that morning and, if it hadn't have been for Sarah's warning, I would have passed on cleaning up the Harbor Cafe and just snoozed on the pier with Jim. Instead, I stayed to work for Mr. O'Neill and after lunch, I mopped up the floor and stood at the door waiting for it to dry while gazing out at the water. A movement down the dock caught my attention and I saw Sheriff Murphy headed toward me. He hesitated when he caught my glance, and then continued toward me.

"Have you seen the dock manager, Augie?" the sheriff asked.

"Not since noon," I answered. The sheriff thanked me without meeting my eye, and it struck me as odd. I called after him: "Did those folks get buried, Sheriff?"

He wheeled and stared at me, his brow knitted darkly down. "What folks? Who?"

"The Chinese. The Chinese on the beach. You know," I stammered in the face of his vehemence.

"Them. Oh, them. Yeah, Augie. They got buried last evening. Don't you worry about them," he answered and walked off.

The sheriff left me confused. I thought the Chinese were the biggest thing to happen on the island since time immemorial. The dock was abuzz with the news all morning and I had been a minor celebrity for having helped to bring the bodies to the makeshift morgue. When I told the story of Momma giving the last rites with holy oil borrowed from St. Ann's, even some fishermen gathered around me to hear my description. The information that their feet had been bashed to pieces led several men to tell their stories of gory deaths. It was a wonder that any of us could eat at all but, when at mid-morning in my honor as a good Catholic Mr. O'Neill offered free to pie to all comers, as a group we managed to finish off three of his apple concoctions. The storytelling session broke up only when the captain of the trawler rang the bell to shove off. Yet the sheriff had acted as if finding young suicide victims from a country five thousand miles away on our beach was of faint reason to comment.

The afternoon was much slower. One trawler and one small pack boat came in. Jim was called from his reading pier only once, for the pack boat, and there was barely enough money to tip each of us boys who worked.   At four o'clock, I reasoned the day wouldn't be getting any better, and I signaled Jim to go. Just as we reached the end of the dock, the sheriff rounded the corner in his roomy sedan and motioned us to climb in.

"Going home?" he said, tiredly.

We failed to respond, our hands hanging heavily down our sides, and my sack of leftovers dangling toward the ground. A free ride home would normally warrant some enthusiastic scrambling to pull open the car door and thanking the sheriff with deep-throated chortling, but his demeanor unsteadied us. Warning signs were in his unmoving eyebrows and in the way he sat back in the seat, not reaching to open the door, as though he didn't really want us to get in.

"Come on," he slowly gestured. "We'll go home."

We climbed in without speaking, and tried to settle in our seats, as if we could stop the disagreeable by behaving decorously.

"Anything new?" I asked the sheriff awkwardly.

There was silence as the sheriff rounded the corner pulling away from the docks, and set his sedan in the dusty ruts that carved deep into the road home. Jim was in the front seat and I in the back. I caught Jim's profile angled toward our driver. The black shock of hair over his forehead, a black eyebrow arching over a blue eye, the smooth skin with a cherry-colored cheek, a broad cut, chiseled chin line that framed a gentle mouth. At that moment I think he realized what had happened, as he realized many things sooner and better than I did. He blinked several times and then looked straight ahead. I sat back and wondered if we were to be accused of something.

The sheriff dropped any pretense of normality and his next question told me something was terribly wrong.

"Is your mother home, boys?"

"She is," I said. "But Sarah won't be along until six o'clock. Maybe we should wait for her."

"We'll get her now," said the sheriff, and he turned around and headed back to town and to the cannery. Jim said nothing but I thought I saw his back tremble slightly, as though his heart was pounding into it and making it vibrate. Sarah loaded into the back seat with me.

"You boys in some kind of trouble?" she asked.

"It's Pop," Jim said.

She sunk back into the seat and looked out the window. Every feature Jim had, she had, except they were winnowed down to miniature proportions. And perhaps because of that delicacy, her nose looked sharper, more focused and much like Pop's. Her dark hair, left to grow, curled thick, trying to wriggle out of her bun.

"Are you sure?" Jim said to the sheriff.

"I believe so."

I breathed in big gulps of air but didn't seem able to breathe back out again. I made little panting sounds as I tried to get my throat and chest to calm down and work properly. Sarah and Jim didn't talk and didn't look at me. My hands clutched my knees and I stared uselessly out the window.

At the house the sheriff pulled his car off the road and we climbed out in slow motion, none of us sure where to go or what to do. I was the oldest boy and should have stepped into the role of host, but the last thing I wanted to do was present Momma with our guest. The sheriff made his way around to the back of the house himself, and the three of us finally gathered our courage and followed him tearlessly.

Death is not what you think it's going to be. It's not the drama or pain you see in plays and movies when the family and friends cry and wail about what has happened. Death is the aloneness of it all coming at you in a huge cloud, meant only for you. You're in the cloud and can barely see out. The air is scratchy white wool that makes breathing a chore. There's no morning, no sun, no stars, no breeze. Your home goes away and there is just you and your heartbeat.

Momma stepped into that cloud when the sheriff joined her in the kitchen, sat her at the table, and explained that Petesy Corrigan's boat was found wrecked against the west side of Vancouver Island. A storm had come up Saturday night and Pop had radioed for help. He wasn't far off shore but the winds were high, whipping around in a sudden storm trough. It was odd, said the sheriff, because normally the *Carolina* should have been able to handle a short summer storm like that, but somehow they went down and broke in half. Pop and Petesy were the only ones on board. What washed ashore was the pilot room since the weight of the engine pulled the hull of the *Carolina* to the bottom of the sea. Pop and Petesy were gone also, probably washed overboard in the midst of fighting off the storm.

It was quick, the sheriff said, just as the storm had been lightning-quick coming and going. Patrol boats went out in the morning, but there was nothing and no one to be found.

"There's another odd thing I have to ask you about," said the sheriff quietly. I don't think he really expected an answer from Momma, but he went on anyway, maybe just to get the question out, as if he were thinking out loud.

"Did Edward talk much about Petesy's luck at fishing?" asked the Sheriff.

Momma looked directly at the Sheriff but didn't say anything. He continued.

"Petesy always seemed to be just short of a good haul, always looking for money, but there they were, gone all the way up on the north part of Vancouver, and they stayed away from the good fishing holes. When your husband radioed for help, he gave as his location a spot close to the coast that other boats never bothered with."

"Maybe he was blown off course. Maybe he'd done all the fishing he could and was just looking for a quiet place to anchor down for the night," Momma replied.

The tone of Momma's answer made me wonder for a moment if she were angry with the sheriff for bringing this awful news to her, but then I passed it off as fear.

The sheriff took an extra long look at Momma and said he guessed that was probably right. He asked if there was anything he could do, and Momma shrugged and sat back in her chair. She looked down meaninglessly at her hands folded in her lap. Sarah told the sheriff he should let Father O'Hare know what had happened.

We were each stunned into stillness, each in our own cloud of disconnected feelings, and the sheriff's care to gather us all together to receive this news had been unproductive social work. Momma went into her bedroom where Tinker and Jonathan tried to follow but met with a closed door. The rest of us sat scattered around the kitchen table, too unhinged to comment. Jim had the presence of mind to make some oatmeal for Jonathan and Tinker so that they would stop crying for a while. After the sheriff had left to get Father O'Hare, Howard came in the door at a run, and Crayton loped up the back steps a few minutes behind him.

Howard looked around the kitchen desperately and then backed up to lean on the door frame. The silence must have disoriented him. Normally five of us in one room would have set off a hubbub of chattering.

"Did the sheriff talk to Momma?" he finally asked. "I saw his car driving off."

We nodded, somehow unsurprised that he might already know, and his head sagged down.

"Then he told her about the fire?"

We looked at him wonderingly then, as if he hearkened from another world, one that we longed to go to and hide in. One that seemed so tarnished when we were in it, but now looked sunny and pleasant.

There was no answer and he lurched on. "I set a fire down at the beach. Didn't hurt no one."

Howard had, for one last time, a boy's concerns about being caught and punished for his latest prank. Too soon, he would have a young man's concerns about his mother's welfare and his next meal. He thought his future depended upon his father's decision to punish him or not, when, unaccountably, it now depended on our adolescent abilities to earn a living.

Still none of us spoke. It seemed to me then that what Howard most needed was what I could not offer. He needed a Pop to guide him through his latest brush with delinquency, a Pop to hem him in by any means necessary so he would do himself minimum damage. All we could offer him, or ourselves, was a future guided by guesswork, if guided at all. Still none of us spoke.

Crayton came in the door and swept past Howard. Crayton held a bunch of wildflowers and he headed for the sink to fill up a glass with water to use as a vase.

"Jim, I found your favorite blue violet," Crayton began but then fell silent when he saw the rest of us.

"What's wrong?" he asked.

"Momma's crying," said Jonathan between bites of oatmeal.

"Because?" Crayton asked the room in general.

"Pop's drowned in Mr. Corrigan's boat," I said.

"You're lying," shouted Howard. "You're lying and it's not funny."

Howard's fists bunched up and he took a step into the kitchen. He stared defiantly at me.

"I'm going to give it to you, Augie, I don't care. You're lying and it's not funny."

"It's true, Howard. The sheriff said," Jim said quietly.

"You shut up. You just think I'm stupid enough to believe anything. Where's Momma?"

Jonathan banged his spoon against the table and started to cry again.

"She's crying," he sobbed. "I told you she's crying."

Howard's fists relaxed and he looked at Jonathan and then at Sarah.

"It's true," she nodded. "It's true."

Howard walked back to the door and kicked the door frame, then walked outside, sat on the back steps and put his head in his hands. Crayton sat down at the kitchen table with the rest of us, which is just about how Father O'Hare and Mrs. Hanahan found us when they arrived a half hour or so later. The oatmeal was gone and Jonathan had fallen asleep in Sarah's lap, and Crayton was pushing Tinker in the swings. Not a one of us knew what to do.

Father and Mrs. Hanahan went straight up to Momma's room for ten minutes or so. When they came back down the steps Mrs. Hanahan was saying that something had to be done to stop her shaking and Father said he'd go to the doctor and get something. Before he left he told us mostly what we already knew, that a very sad thing had happened and we had some difficult times ahead of us. He added a comment that did help, however. He said that what we should be doing was thinking of jobs our mother would need done and try to do them as best we could.

"Sarah, Augie, you'll be growing up real fast now," he said. "You'll see to the others."

Father headed off toward town, but as an afterthought, turned back and called Howard from the steps and asked him if he wanted to come along and help find the doctor. Howard agreed and set off with him.

Mrs. Hanahan had brought some beef brisket with her and a head of cabbage and set to making a stew with Sarah's help. She told Jim and me that plenty of people would be in and out of the house in the next few days and we should start dusting and sweeping any and every surface. Crayton, she said, would be in charge of Tinker and Jonathan. We laid Jonathan and Tinker in bed and got to work.

The next days unfolded pretty much as Mrs. Hanahan had predicted. Church members filed in an out of the house, and even a few Protestants who knew Pop from fishing or card playing paid Momma their respects. Pop's two half-sisters were still living in Pennsylvania, and Father asked Jim to write them a telegram. Momma's family in Ireland would have to wait for a letter to be sent many weeks later.

Mrs. Hanahan said that not having a body to bury meant not having a wake, and that made everything so much harder. She had me go to Mr. Kilgore's and make a deal to pay a little down for a coffin, and promise to pay the rest later, so we would have something to bury. Mr. Kilgore produced another simple pine coffin, and Father O'Hare agreed to say a Mass and bless the coffin in lieu of the usual funeral.

The memorial service was held on Thursday, and from Tuesday to Saturday, neighbors came and went with food and drink so frequently that for the first time that I could remember we had a surplus of food. We didn't own a refrigerator and we kept our food in the dry pantry. Up until then, the only perishable food we bought was a little meat that would be cooked the same day and milk and butter, which was delivered six days a week ice-cold from the creamery and kept in a bucket of cold water. Father O'Hare brought us an ice chest and made it Howard's job to go to town each day and buy a block of ice so that the leftover food would not go to waste.

Momma took the medicine that the doctor sent and seemed to stumble through the following days as a barely audible presence. She could hear us, and acknowledged us with a nod and sometimes even a smile, but she formed few words to tell us how she felt or thought about the damage a north wind off Vancouver Island had done to our family. I'd wake up each morning wondering if that would be the day someone would explain things to me, explain how Pop could wash to the bottom of the sea and not come back.

Sometimes, lying in my bed I would remember the Chinese couple on the beach nearly in shreds. I would wish Pop would come up on Beacon Beach somehow intact and we could find him and Momma could put holy oil on his head just to say goodbye.

Other times, to make it more bearable, I imagined him inside the hull of the boat, tucked in his bunk and sleeping forever, happy to be resting and not working.

That's the story I told Crayton, Jonathan and Tinker over and over again until I almost believed it, too. We thought he was lost, I said, but really he had found the place he most wanted to be.

Maybe I didn't fully believe that story and I wished my Pop had not been on the *Carolina* but he was and I needed to find the logic of it. His and Petesy's bad luck made me cry alone at night. I wished them back fiercely over and over again, and I wished somehow I had been on the dock the day they left to warn them about the dangers. I would have spoken about the weather, or the need for more crew. I would have pointed out that I was making money and I would be working all summer all day long and able to earn quite a bit. In truth, I knew they wouldn't have listened to a young fellow with silly fears, and I could see Petesy laughing and pushing off with an easy wave. He meant no harm to my Pop, I thought, and now he shared a fate somewhere in the ocean with my father.

In my mind, Pop's honor and Petesy's honor became linked, and I got the idea that we should mark that link. Forgetting Petesy would be like forgetting part of the story of my own father's death. I brought the idea to the sheriff. After the church service and the burial of our empty coffin, he and I were walking back from the cemetery behind St. Ann's to his car where Momma waited with Sarah to go home.

"Pop got some kind of funeral, even without a body," I ruminated. "What about Petesy Corrigan? He was Catholic, too. He needs something."

"He's got no folks left," replied the sheriff. "His family that's left is all somewhere in Ohio."

"Still," I persisted, "that's an even better reason. Somebody should say some prayers for him. I'll talk to Momma." I strode faster toward the car and the sheriff's arm shot out to hold me back.

"Your Momma can't hear that now, Augie," he blurted.

"It'll be good for her to think of someone else. She's strong enough." I turned toward the car again.

"Look, Petesy Corrigan wasn't what he always seemed to be, Augie. Your Momma knows that and I guarantee this is not the time to go talking about him with her."

"It wasn't Petesy's fault there was a storm. Sure, he could have had a better boat, but that's the way it was and it was bad luck all around," I said.

"It was bad luck, yes, but Petesy made some of his bad luck himself. Now don't go upsetting your mother. I'll talk to Father O'Hare and he'll say a Mass for Petesy if it'll make you feel better. Just don't bring up the subject with your mother."

We had nearly reached the car and the sternness of the sheriff's tone must have filtered into the car. Momma was watching us with a glaze of suspicion in her eyes.

"If Pop is worth a funeral, why isn't Petesy?" I argued.

Sarah scowled through the glass as if to keep any unsettling discussions outside their protective shell.

"Stand up straight and keep your Momma well," said the sheriff, and clapped me on the back as if we were having a regular conversation. I got in the car and he drove us home in silence.

Twelve

Searching for Trees and Finding the Forest

Sarah was the first of us to come to her senses and start making plans beyond the roasts and pies that the neighbors brought us to tide us over. We had pretty much lived from Pop's work as a navigator and that was gone for good.

Sarah, Jim and I had made some meager contributions from our summer and weekend jobs. Momma kept a garden that supplied us with vegetables, and in season we had apples and pears from the yard and blackberries from the acres of bushes that grew wild on the island. Beyond those paltry resources, we hadn't enough to keep a family of eight fed and clothed without Pop's earnings.

"You can't go back to school in September, Augie," Sarah decided the day after Pop's memorial service. "We both have to work now, even if it means leaving the island to find a better job."

I thought she was crazy, talking about leaving home, but leaving school didn't sound half bad. I had already done all the arithmetic, geometry and grammar that the teachers seemed to know at our little high school, and I could leave the novels and poetry they thought were so beautiful to Jim. He understood them better than I did anyway.

Sarah had graduated in June, and kept on at her job. When she let them know she would be continuing in September, the cannery supervisor began to let her learn more of the processing and some of the business recordkeeping. Momma had hoped that Sarah would go to business school in Anacortes and learn to be a secretary or some vocation more uplifting than shoving salmon into a tin, but none of us had much choice.

For my part, both the Harbor Cafe and the hardware store had work available, but not enough to keep eight bodies and souls together, so Mr. O'Neill and Mr. Conawalski and I pieced together an arrangement whereby I worked at both places, with an agreement that if one place needed me more than another a certain week, I could shift hours accordingly.

Having one boss is trouble enough, so two of them telling me what to do and when to do it made me hit the bed at night earlier than my brothers and with less in my stomach. On the other hand, I was now seldom bored and got to learn two businesses at the same time from different points of view, not to mention the fact that as an employee I stood a good chance of gaining entry to the Sunday poker games in the back of Mr. Conawalski's store.

Mornings found me at the cafe preparing the food for lunch. At about two in the afternoon I'd head over to the hardware store and work until six or so. Mr. Conawalski had me keep his warehouse in order and I soon got to know each bolt size and shape like the cards in a deck. The sudden change from schoolboy to working man meant fewer hours with my brothers, and I missed the familiarity of their teasing. Jim would drop in to see how I was doing on his way from school to the library where Miss Paletto had offered him a few hours work each week shelving books.

"How's the job going?" I asked him one afternoon.

"Can't complain," Jim answered. "Miss Paletto gives me plenty of books to shelve, but when I'm done I get to sit in any stack I like and just read."

"But is your homework getting done?" I replied.

"It's no good to try to be my Pop, Augie." He smiled lightly at me. "And Pop would never have asked that question anyway."

While I didn't like the reply, the sight of his smile, rarer and rarer since Pop was gone, made me pass it over.

"OK, well I just don't want to hear of any problems," I grumbled. "Is Howard getting his homework done?"

"Howard thinks homework is for sissies," he grinned. "And the teachers think Howard is for the birds, so it comes out to be a fair trade."

"You're in a cheery mood. What's the news with you?"

"I found a book, Augie, a book with a great poem in it," he explained.

How good could a poem be, I wondered to myself, when the weather is perfect for fishing off the pier and I am stuck in here sorting nails? A poem, great or poor, could not fix the bother of working for a living. But I feared Jim would not visit me so often if I didn't keep up my end of the conversation, so I acted interested.

"Let's see," I put down the nail jar and took a step to the stool where he was resting, watching me sift through a pile of one penny to ten penny nails all in a jumble.

"The book is in the library," he admitted.

"We'll leave it for another day, then," I said with some relief.

"I know it by heart—well, at least part," Jim said hurriedly. "Listen."

He began to recite, more smoothly than I can name my own brothers and sisters, words I barely perceived as English the first time through. When he was done he sat still, looking at me. His smile was gone but his look was as peaceful as the sunset over our apple trees.

I opened my mouth to ask him to repeat whatever it was he said that had given him such calm after weeks of drifting melancholy and a tired distance from all but the most critical chores of living. Before I could ask, however, Mr. Conawalski opened the door to the storeroom from the front of the shop and gave me what I had begun to know as the "evil eye." Jim got the message fast enough and stood up from the stool and said he had to get going to the library.

"Part-time only works, Augie, if you give it the full-time spirit," my boss said for about the hundredth time since I had started working for him.

Truly, Mr. Conawalski had done me a large favor by finding me employment at his business, but his enthusiastic encouragement of my entry into the working world was starting to wear me down almost before I had begun. Why owners believe that employees can be made as interested as they are in their profits still escapes me to this day, but Mr. Conawalski was bound and determined to do so.

"Nails sorted are nails sold," he heartily reminded me as Jim left through the warehouse door to the alley, winking back at me through the window before he ambled off to the library.

I admired my boss' industry, his patience with customers, his neatness and care of his property. My role as stalwart protector of that property had been mightily impressed upon me and I accepted it as such, a role I had to take in order to bring home my pay. Nonetheless, I could not embrace such a role with the exuberance Mr. Conawalski expected.

"I've been timing you," he said after Jim had left, "and you sort faster when the nails are put into boxes instead of jars. So from now on, let's arrange the boxes on the shelf and save the jars for the really small items, like washers. You could be doing twice the work you're doing now." He beamed at me.

I swallowed hard, trying to find a suitable answer. Mr. Conawalski was suspicious.

"Maybe not twice as fast but one and half, anyway. Wouldn't that be good?" he tested me.

"Very good. I'm sure it will work," I answered.

"You needn't be sad about it," he huffed. "The sooner you sort the sooner you can get back out front and learn the more interesting jobs."

"Interesting?" I said, trying to be ambitious, but evidently sounding somewhat sarcastic.

"Yes, interesting," he said, irritated. "Like putting in the order for new boat line, and keeping the tool inventory up to date. There are a lot of different screwdrivers available and you ought to know about them."

I emptied the nails out of the jars, put the boxes on the shelf, and started sorting again in earnest. I smiled at my boss and tried to employ my whole face in the effort. He sighed and returned to the front of the store. He was left, I imagined, with the same sense of failure I had.

The work at Mr. O'Neill's cafe had a different tone to it. It was dirtier work, mopping and wiping away the trails of rough-cut sailors. They ate gallons of stew, which meant piles of potato peelings and vegetable scraps to be gathered up and fed to the chickens and hogs he kept in pens outside the kitchen door. The cutting boards had to be scraped clean and bleached every day, but only after scrubbing the burnt gristle off a dozen or so pots and pans.

The work was made bearable by Mr. O'Neill's admission that it was pointless, thankless labor that was to be repeated day in and day out until he reached his grave. He would clap me on the back, swear at my slowness, and promise me a piece of pie once the livestock was fed. He laughed at my jokes and treated me like I had the brains of any other man he had ever laid eyes on.

Handling the two worlds of the hardscrabble cafe and the earnest hardware store kept me busy at a time when too much thinking would have served little purpose. At night, I would fall into a deep sleep before the lights in our room went off, snoring like a sea lion, Crayton swore. I was healthy and grew a new girth of muscles from my shoulders down to my ankles. A customer at the hardware store startled me by calling out "Hey, mister" to get my attention. Only in the mornings, as I woke and remembered what the day would bring and why, would the common sense of things be hard to grasp.

The doubts about what really happened to my father had been washing over me since my conversation with the sheriff at the cemetery. While Pop had the remembrance of a headstone at the cemetery, Petesy Corrigan was washed to sea with nary a comment from any soul in Friday Harbor. Momma's lack of interest in Petesy Corrigan's death, or in what had become of his possessions, struck me as odd, but maybe she was too distracted to care. Other fishermen, however, would be expected to discuss the storm, or evaluate the safety features, or lack thereof, on Petesy's boat—if not with concern toward Petesy, at least with an eye to having his misfortune inform their own practices. Instead, the silence around the tragedy was stony and complete, to the point, I thought, of nervous avoidance. In my presence, the local fishermen seemed to hesitate mentioning even the lightest squall—let alone any heavier weather that might recall the rogue storm that sank the *Carolina*.

Then in October, when I had enough money to make a small payment to Mr. Kilgore for Pop's coffin, it turned out that someone had already paid for it.

"Who?" I asked. I was perplexed.

"Don't know if you don't know. I got an envelope under the door. Just assumed it was one of you," Mr. Kilgore replied with a shrug.

Momma didn't look up from kneading bread when I told her.

"Probably someone from the church," she muttered.

"Who would have that kind of extra money? Unless Mr. Corrigan had some money in the bank and they wanted to give it to us to use," I offered.

"Petesy? Extra money? Why, that's an idea..." Momma started with a sudden shrillness and then cut her comments off with no explanation. "Go find Tinker and make sure she gets a bath," she said more gently.

"That is Crayton's job," I answered

, not wanting to be distracted. I wanted to know more about Momma's estimation of Petesy and exactly how his life had come to intersect with ours.

"Fine. Go and see to it that he gets it done," she answered and turned to the sink, letting her back close off further conversation.

I dropped the matter because actually I was glad to have the bit of extra cash. I had, as I'd anticipated, gotten Mr. Conawalski to admit me to the Sunday afternoon poker game, and I needed some ready money. That same Sunday, when Mr. Kilgore declared the coffin paid for, I got in the game. I was very nervous about playing with the men and not my schoolmates, and I played clumsily. I was down to my last fifty cents when Mr. Conawalski had to step away from the game.

"Don't bet 'til I get back," he said in a condescending tone that rankled me.

By the time he returned one round later I was five dollars in debt to Ammie Kilgore's uncle, Jack Madsen.

"You got the boy in a corner," Mr. Conawalski said when he rejoined the circle of players.

"Says he's going to sell me his father's gold watch," Jack answered.

"Not this round, he's not," Mr. Conawalski retorted. "You're done, Augie. I'll cover your losses."

I left, both bereft of my dignity and mightily relieved with Mr. Conawalski's decision, because my father hadn't owned any gold watch, or at least, if he did he certainly had not bequeathed it to me. If he had, however, I would have given it up gladly rather than sacrifice five dollars from my next pay envelope, which is what I thought the thrifty Mr. Conawalski would surely do to recoup his five dollars.

But he didn't dock my pay, and in fact never brought it up again. When I tried to say something, he looked at me severely, and I dropped the subject.

Charity towards a family that had just lost its head of the household should have seemed natural to me, but in my new role as chief wage earner, it rankled me. Pop's pride had left its mark and I was determined to provide well for my sisters and brothers so that no one would be tempted to interfere in our family. Also, I must admit, in the back of my mind was the less noble purpose of regaining respect and being readmitted to the Sunday card game.

The coming of winter gave me a chance to rebuild my reputation. We would need firewood. If I provided for that need, and my family did not have to borrow, I was sure my manhood would be established in the eyes of every adult, and every card player, in town.

At work, at both places, I asked everyone who happened by if they had or knew of felled trees that Jim and I could cut up. Nobody I spoke to knew of anything but green wood that wouldn't burn right until the following year. I had all but begun to panic when Mr. O'Neill suggested I comb the west side of the island near Beacon Beach where the wind always hit the hardest.

"Surely there's a tree or two along those godforsaken cliffs that's been down a while," he said. "Look, you go scouting and find 'em, and I'll scare up another fellow, and together we'll all move 'em out for you."

I must have looked as though my pride was injured, once again accepting outside help, so Mr. O'Neill added on the convincing argument.

"You and your brother will be doing the cutting and splitting and carrying, we'll just give you a hand with the transportation. Kilgore owes me a favor and I bet he'll lend me his truck. You boys'll be the muscle. I'll just be working the gas pedal."

For the next two Sunday afternoons, I scoured the areas on the windward side of the island. Although I needed to stay close to Beacon Beach, since that was the one place Mr. Kilgore's truck could reach, walking there alone was harrowing. Warmer than normal air formed a fitful fog that would come and go like visiting spirits. The open beach was the perfect receiving ground for memories from the sea, and I scampered over it like a colt with a prod at its back.

I slowed down and started my search at the north end of the beach, towards the jutting ledges of Shore Heights. Mr. O'Neill suggested

I'd find trees down all the way north to Point Tear Drop, a corner of land that extended out into the water in a graceful, rounded formation that gave it its name.

That first Sunday, I had to fight my way through heavy brush and punishing thistles from the edge of Beacon Beach up the rocky shore to just under Shore Heights. I spotted one good-size tree that was down, and looked cured but not yet punky from too much wet weather. It was a good tree, but not enough to keep us warm all winter long. All the other felled trees were either too skinny, green or rotted.

Dark was falling earlier than I expected, and the sun in its October flame of glory was setting into the wet horizon. I headed back out of the brush and loped homeward, my back to the sea and its implied threats.

The next Sunday I returned and made more decisive headway through the brush. I reached Shore Heights and my tree fairly quickly. I bent down to turn it over, just to make sure this lumber would be worth cutting. When I rolled it away from me, the tree's length turned, and pressed down the long, hovering ferns that had grown around it. The movement revealed a marked path cut through the brush and carefully bordered with fist-sized stones.

Hunters, I thought. Deer or raccoon hunters who had found a particularly useful blind might hope to keep it marked. I followed along the string of stones, kicking back some of the fast-growing ferns and vines, until it reached the base of the cliff below Shore Heights. There the thread of stones ended, and dirt and rock melded into one and heaved upwards at about an eighty-degree angle. It seemed like a dead end so I turned back toward the beach, foraging as I walked for a good hiking stick.

When I shoved aside some green branches from the side of the bushy, rocky cliff ascending before me, a brightly colored ribbon appeared. It was tied to a branch of the bush, as were three more behind it. I broke off an overhanging tree branch nearby and shoved it down beyond the ribbons into the dirt under the bushes, thinking I'd hear and feel the snap of a raccoon trap. Instead my stick snagged the coil of a thick rope and as I pulled it toward me, the bushes above rustled slowly. I had found the lower end of a heavy climbing rope that, as I pulled it, snaked out from the brush until it went taut. I could see it led a good way up the steep hill to Shore Heights. Someone had rigged a climbing path up the incline.

I dropped the stick, grabbed the rope, and hand over hand, ascended the brushy hill. The first rope ran out at the base of a tree around which it was securely knotted. The next rope, tied off at the same tree, led me across and up the hill to another tree and another rope. So I continued until I had climbed to the base of the jutting rocks of Shore Heights.

A rope, evidently secured inside the cave, hung down to my precarious position. It was supported by a tree sunk deep in the soil, but tipped downwards towards the rocky shore and the choppy waters. This last rope had thick knots that allowed me to shimmy up onto the ledge of the cave. Standing on the outer point of Shore Heights, the view was magnificent. Like the prow of an enormous ship, the ledge hung over the shore.

Just three months earlier, I would have felt I had discovered a treasure greater than pirate's gold. I could have led Jim and Crayton here for secret games. Even Howard might have been impressed. But now alone, with the day waning and sunless breezes whispering along the damp walls of the cave, I reminded myself of the importance of firewood. I used the vantage point to search below for felled trees that could be cut and dragged away. My eyes scanned the areas along the shore, and I noticed that towards the north the brush thinned out, the sandy strip of beach widened, and a number of thick trees lay scattered. Perhaps they had been washed up by the tide. I scrambled back down the rope ladder and let myself down the incline.

The same path that had led me to the rope climb took me back to the shore and then twisted sharply north. I followed it until the brush thinned out and sand took over more of the woods. The path became a narrow skirt of beach. The water-logged trees I had seen from the ledge were scattered like huge, unsharpened pencils, washed clean of bark and discarded by the inattentive waves.

I hopped from one candidate to another. With a pen knife, I dug into tree after tree to test the wood's strength and water content. The trees seemed mostly solid, with just a light outer layer of salt-softened pulp. The prospect of profits to be made from this wood powered up my muscles and I worked my way north rapidly. I started to think my brother and I might cut enough wood to sell to other families. By the time I reached the end of the beach at Tear Drop Point, my arms ached from rolling and stabbing the drenched logs. I sat heavily on the sand and leaned back against a driftwood trunk and closed my eyes. I must have napped just briefly, but enough to blur the purpose of my hike, because when I woke up I jumped to my feet, trying to get my bearings.

On the one side of the bushes and rocks that served to form a natural end to the narrow beach, the land curved out into the water in its teardrop shape. The teardrop itself was made of large, flat and elongated rocks, easy to climb on. The curve of the rock formation formed a small cove where the water lapped calmly. On the other side of that row of bushes, I saw for the first time that the land dipped down into a kind of sandy valley. The large ditch was a triangle of protected space snuggled into the base of the cliffs that rose behind me. At the bottom of the space, the damp sand had been stamped down, and a circle of rocks formed a fireplace around the dry, fresh remains of a coal fire.

I half slid, half tumbled down the side of this inverted dune and landed uncomfortably on an unbending surface. My hand felt under me for a rock but pulled out a metal fuel can. It held what I guessed was the source of ignition for the coal fire. The can had a narrow, short spout and looked like it held about a quart of kerosene.

I turned it over, heard the splash of liquid inside, and read the name *Carolina* scratched on its flat underside.

I rubbed the word with my thumb in an effort to rearrange the letters into something more comprehensible or at least, less alarming. The word, however, stayed firmly etched into the tin.

It felt as if the sandy hole might close up around me. It was a trap, a trick, a ghost's encampment, or even the devil's lair. The *Carolina* was at the bottom of the ocean, and only a supernatural event, could, I believed, have brought back this artifact from the deep. I flung the can away from me and hurtled up the embankment, back on to the sand and on a run southward to Beacon Beach. Holding the fuel can in my hands was like handling an object from my father's grave, and that thought kept me moving instinctively, irrationally, unstoppably as far away and as quickly away as possible.

As I ran I swore that some of the shrubs moved toward me, reaching for me. Others shivered, as if they knew what dangers lay ahead. I started to zigzag through the brush, hoping to foil the snares I was sure were placed to capture me. Finally, I burst out onto the beach and looked back at the scraggy growth made ghostly by the white fog. It seemed to stare back, disappointed by my escape. I trotted briskly off the beach and onto the road home, slowly feeling my senses collect.

By the time I reached home I had calmed myself enough to consider the possibility that the sandy den had been an exaggeration, a kind of mirage prompted by the dreams of my nap. Maybe the scrawl on the fuel can spelled a different name than the one I thought I saw.

Thirteen

Doubts

For most of the next week I kept my adventures out at Beacon Beach to myself, but the specter would not fade. I had to return. I had already promised Momma heaps of firewood, and so she had been burning our reserve wood with little concern. We knew that after Halloween temperatures would drop sharply and the storm season would set in. She was counting on her boys to bring home more fuel, and I couldn't let her down. I couldn't admit to her or my brothers that I was haunted by what might exist in the woods and beaches, and I was bullied into facing it by my own pride.

At work at the cafe on Monday, Mr. O'Neill asked about my progress and we decided that he should arrange to have Mr. Kilgore's truck the following Sunday.

"You'll have enough cut to bring out?" he asked.

"It won't be split, but it'll be in rounds," I answered. "If I can have Saturday off to cut with Jim."

"Take Friday and Saturday," Mr. O'Neill said. "I don't want to have to go out there twice."

Tuesday morning at breakfast, Jim had seventy reasons for why he could not miss school on Friday, but Howard had none, and together we convinced him he needed to pitch in and saw up enough trees to see us through the winter. Howard, in fact, thought we would be better off to begin on Tuesday, but I convinced him that my jobs still came before firewood. We could be cold, I said, but we couldn't afford not to eat.

"Yeah, and we could afford to eat more, too," Howard tossed out. "I don't see why I can't just work the docks, instead of going to that stupid school. I'm turning fourteen next month and I look sixteen. It's a waste for me to be pushing a pencil across some lousy piece of paper when I could be bringing in good money."

"School until you're sixteen, and that's the rule," I intoned.

"Whose rule?"

"Momma...and Pop's rule."

"Yeah, like he would have cared. And Momma won't care either when she sees that Tinker's bones aren't even growing because she doesn't get enough meat," Howard scowled at me. "Well, I don't care. That's a rule that's gonna be broken and we'll see who stops me."

We had been over this territory before and Howard's thick-headedness was beginning to wear on me. I started to appreciate Pop's assaults on our will.

"If you know what's good for you, you'll stop yapping so much and just do what your mother asks you to," I snapped. Howard scowled some more and swallowed his last spoonful of oatmeal. Momma came into the kitchen with Crayton, Jonathan and Tinker in tow.

"Yeah, sure, Augie," Howard said, lightening his tone. "And by the way, the milkman asked me yesterday when we thought we could pay last month's bill." He smiled at me evenly and lifted his eyebrows with meaning. He grabbed his books, said goodbye, and left for school.

Momma started another pan of oatmeal for her second batch of customers, but shifted from one foot to another in the heavy silence that fell over the breakfast table after Howard's departure. I stared at the fire and Jim pushed his oatmeal around his bowl with a spoon. Crayton and the smaller ones started their morning chatter about who would use which bowl and which cup, but even they quieted under the spell of worry that Howard had left in his wake. As I stood to leave, Jim heaved a sigh and shifted in his place.

"I'll start work in February, Augie. I'll turn sixteen then. I can go full-time on the docks."

I am not sure, that in the years I've lived since that morning, I've heard words more burdened with the ache of sacrifice. Jim looked at me bravely and nodded his head, as though the decision had been made and confirmed. Momma turned and looked at me from the stove, and for just a flash, both agreement and remorse fought for control of her expression. Her steady voice, nevertheless, betrayed none of it when she spoke.

"Not while I'm breathing," Momma sang out. "There's no creditor that can't stand to wait, but an education can't be put off. Sarah has her diploma, and Augie is just taking a little break now while we get stabilized. But that's it. Everybody else stays in school."

"Subject closed," I said.

"We'll see," said Jim, softly, but the clouds in his eyes had broken up and dispersed. Momma smiled for an extra moment longer than usual at me and then filled the bowls of Crayton, Jonathan and Tinker. I put on my jacket and left for town and the mounds of potatoes I would peel that day on my "break" from school.

As usual, the hours at the cafe trotted along at a steady pace, and the day began to drag at Mr. Conawalski's world of careful counting and categorizing. The best relief for the tedium of sorting and warehousing thousands of utilitarian objects was visiting with customers whenever I got the chance. As I began to learn more about the store, Mr. Conawalski let me work behind the counter for short turns when he needed to go down the street to the bank or on some other errand.

On Monday and Tuesday while Mr. Conawalski was gone, the customers were a steady stream of friendly faces, many of them women from St. Ann's Parish who knew Momma and were generous with their praise and encouragement of my new career.

"You're your mother's saving grace," said Mrs. Hartford. "I'll be sending my Mike to talk to you soon. It's about time he got serious, too."

Mrs. Doyle, a neighbor who had more than once chased Sarah and me away from her plum trees with a stick, was equally fulsome. "He's a man now, Mary," she addressed herself to Mrs. Hartford. "He'll be marrying one of the Conawalski girls before you know it." They both beamed knowingly at me, and I was obliged to smile back, although my spirits sank at the easy way they doomed me to the dullest life I could imagine.

On Wednesday, when Mr. Conawalski took a box of plaster to the grocery store for some repairs they needed, Mrs. Conawalski came in. She bustled in as if her visit were being timed by an efficiency expert, and came straight towards me, inquiring for her husband as she walked.

"He stepped over to the grocer's for a moment. Should be right back," I answered and voluntarily began to sort the nuts from the washers in the odds and ends bin at the end of the counter. As I feared she might, Mrs. Conawalski discovered a job for herself.

"What an amount of dust has accumulated on these shelves here," she exclaimed. She set her hat and gloves on the counter, came behind to where I stood, and plucked the feather duster from a hook under the counter where Mr. Conawalski had carefully stored all his cleaning implements.

"It's such a good feeling to keep everything neat and tidy, isn't it?" she said as she fluttered the duster rapidly from shelf to shelf behind one counter and along the perimeter of the next. "Mr. Conawalski loves a neat home, and I do try to keep it that way, not that it's so large that I can't, but it does take some thinking about it, and now with the girls in school, well, I can see that the chores get done, although they do keep me busy with sewing the dresses they need, and their school projects, and all those things you busy young people are doing these days."

I guessed it was part of my job to be respectful of the Conawalski family and so I politely continued the conversation.

"Your girls like school, don't they?" I asked.

"Well, of course, they have their ideas about which teachers are doing their best and which are just earning a living, and I tell them that sometimes you just have to take it upon yourself to teach yourself and make the best of things but if they don't see a reason for reading a certain book I just can't convince them so I wish the teachers sometimes would be a little more forceful about requiring things but my girls seem to be learning more than most."

I thought of Jim's comment that discussing Shakespeare with one of the Conawalski girls was like going fishing without a pole, and I just smiled to myself.

Mrs. Conawalski was continuing on with her comments when one of the tradesmen from town came in, a man I knew only by sight. I turned to serve him, and Mrs. Conawalski brought her duster to a halt.

"Wally around?" he asked.

"He'll be back soon. Something I can do?"

"I came to pay on my account. Got paid for a job and I better put it down on my debt here before I spend it." He smiled.

"Well, sure I'll be glad to take your money, but I don't know about any account book." I hesitated.

"Silly, it's in the drawer there," Mrs. Conawalski burst out, heading towards my place at the counter.

"That one, there," she pointed under the cash register.

"But that drawer is always locked, and I don't have the key," I said.

"Oh, you young folks," she continued. "If it weren't for those of us with a little experience, what would become of you?"

She laughed in that frenetic way she had, then slipped her hand under the counter to the left of the register, and brought out a key. She handed it to me gaily and strode back to her dusting.

I opened the drawer and found it occupied by a bound and worn-looking dark brown book. Lettered tabs protruded from the side of it indicating an alphabetical organization. I asked the customer's name and opened the book at the letter "C".

"Cotter, Cotter, Cotter," I said as my finger ran down the left column, going from page to page. A line began with a last name, followed by a first name, and then across the columns of the book subsequent spaces aligned for twelve monthly entries. Each name line was followed by four blank lines, so that the book allowed for five years of account records for each customer. As I scanned for Mr. Cotter's record, I wondered what the Mohan family record might look like and I thought I might secretly examine the book some other day when I might be left alone at the front counter.

The pages of names and figures were beginning to blur as I sped up my search for the waiting Mr. Cotter.

"Can't find it, Augie?" pressed the restless Mrs. Conawalski from her dustless corner at the end of the counter.

"I think I have it, now. Let's see, Connor, Connor, gee, there're four Connors and here we go, it's..."

My voice caught in my throat, so that Mrs. Conawalski took a step towards me. My finger had stopped suddenly on the customer right above Cotter. Petesy Corrigan's lines were solid with entries, and the last one was in fresh-looking bright blue ink with the date of September 1936.

Confused, I looked up unseeingly at the arrangement of shelves, counters, tables, bins, jars and hooks that made up the hardware store. The customer drew nearer the counter and leaned over towards me.

"It's Cotter. C-O-T-T-E-R," he intoned helpfully.

"Sure, sure," I said, and looked down at the book, not seeing Cotter, Corrigan, or any name for that fact, just a page of different shades of blue figures fighting the waves of columns that seemed to try to trap and drown them.

I heard Mrs. Conawalski's cheery greeting as the door opened.

"Wally, you're back. Good. I think Augie needs help deciphering your account book. Mr. Cotter here would like to make a payment and we got out the book and of course I didn't want to interfere with your employee's responsibilities so Augie is trying to find the right place himself but I think since it's his first time he might need a little instruction from you, Wally."

Mrs. Conawalski must have left Mr. Conawalski breathless because he appeared at my side wordlessly and took the book from my hand. As he firmly closed it, I awkwardly stepped away. He cleared his throat and smiled at Mr. Cotter, who stood somewhat bemused at his unsuccessful effort to pay a debt. Without breaking his courteous engagement with Mr. Cotter, Mr. Conawalski shoved the account book back in the drawer, locked it, and deposited the key in his pocket.

"Thanks, Augie, for your help," he said without turning his head toward me.

"I'll record your payment in my current account book," he nodded to Mr. Cotter.

Mr. Conawalski took the cash from Mr. Cotter, counted it, and deposited it in his cash register. He looked only at the money and Mr. Cotter, as though they were the only two people in the room. When Mr. Cotter slipped out the door to the street, I pulled in my stomach, inflated my lungs with all available air, and opened my mouth to ask why the supposedly old account book showed a recent receipt of funds from Petesy, who, after all, was currently dead.

But Mr. Conawalski drew a fountain pen from his shirt pocket, and looked sternly at me.

"I can take care of this now."

I breathed out in a deflated rush and Mrs. Conawalski coughed demurely. He looked at her evenly.

"I thought the girls were having an early dinner tonight because of the piano recital," he said with the finality of an order.

Mrs. Conawalski shifted her handbag an inch or so up her forearm, then brushed her hand across her cheek as if to lessen the sting of a slap. The air crackled with our silence.

"I'll go sort some things," I said, and I took several steps backward, toward the storeroom.

Mr. Conawalski leaned over the counter, marking up some packing slips, and took no ostensible notice of either of us

"You have a good day," I heard Mrs. Conawalski say in a near whisper.

I thought to wish the same to her but she swept out the front door with only a barely audible "Goodbye, everyone."

In the cool, shadowy warehouse I went to my sorting bench. I thought if I returned to my routine somehow this new development would clarify itself for me. Mr. Conawalski left me alone for the rest of the afternoon, but my thoughts were still in a knot. I could not come up with an explanation of how Mr. Conawalski could be keeping the record of a dead man's account. I decided to bring the subject up again, even if it wasn't exactly my business.

At closing time, as usual, I went to the front of the store to take my leave. Mr. Conawalski was unboxing a new supply of faucets and arranging a few of them in display on a shelf. He looked up stiffly when I approached him, as though he were still angry at me. I wasn't sure what I had done wrong, but after years of dealing with Pop, I had learned it was better to apologize first and justify yourself afterwards.

"I'm sorry if I disturbed your account book," I said.

"It is the heart of this business. That's why it's under lock and key. No matter what anyone tells you, please do not touch what I have locked up," he answered, his brow deeply furrowed.

"I won't but..." I started my justification. Mr. Conawalski would have none of it.

"You need Friday off to cut wood, correct?" he continued.

"Yes, sir," I said.

"Take tomorrow off, too, then. I don't have as much work as I anticipated, and it would be better if you didn't work so many hours this week."

Stunned and worried, my brow furrowed almost as deeply as his. I had thought that Mr. O'Neill and Mr. Conawalski would consult each other before changing my hours. I wasn't prepared for having one employer reduce my pay without the other employer increasing it. Any decrease in my earnings would have a serious effect at home. I could see Howard rubbing his hands now as he prepared to skip school and work at the docks. Neither Momma nor I would have much reason to stop him. I turned to leave, not wanting Mr. Conawalski to curtail my work schedule any further.

"Augie," he called when I was at the door. I turned to him.

"Sometimes, success at work is as much about thinking as it is about doing," he called, ominously.

I nodded my head in assent and left. Once home, I didn't mention the problem at the hardware store, my reduced hours, or Petesy's account. Trouble, it seemed to me, was something that grew worse with discussion.

I had little choice but to use the unexpected free time the next afternoon sawing the downed tree trunks at Beacon Beach. After work at the cafe, I sharpened our saw on the stone Mr. O'Neill used for his large kitchen knives. I took my time since I didn't relish another afternoon alone on what I had begun to fear as a haunted beach.

Out on the road leading from the docks west to the beach, I passed Ammie Kilgore on his way back to school after lunch. Without much hard work, I persuaded him to play hooky and help me cut up some trees. With the two of us, the long saw would be much more manageable and effective. Maybe, I told him, we'd work up such a sweat we would have to take a swim in the still warm October sunshine.

I was so relieved to not have to return to Beacon Beach alone that I didn't care if Ammie decided to swim all afternoon and not work a lick.

But Ammie was a better worker than I expected. I led him to the bounty I had discovered, and the two of us cut through one long tree in less than an hour. We were done with the better part of a second when we decided to take a break. I had some lunch leftovers from the cafe, and we sat facing the ocean with our backs supported by a log. The cliffs rose behind us and Shore Heights rested heavily over the water to the north.

We talked about his Pa's shop, and the way Ammie was learning to give haircuts by practicing on his dog, and occasionally on his father, and that the dog actually made a better customer. Ammie said he figured cutting one thing or another would be his work for the rest of his life, so taking off from school to help me was really part of training for his future.

"But you'll be the undertaker, too," I reminded him. "There's more than cutting in that job."

"Sure, cleaning and dressing, but there's no trick in that. No, it's the cutting that takes talent."

"What do undertakers cut, anyway?" I asked.

"You cut their hair and nails to make 'em look better. And you have to cut a little bit to get their insides cleaned out. It's the part I don't like. It makes cutting trees seem like fun."

Ammie was a good fellow, I thought then, and not quite the prisoner of conceit I had taken him for. I stood up and motioned towards Tear Drop Cove.

"If I show you something, you won't think I'm crazy?"

"Can't guarantee it," he said. "But I'll try not to burst out laughing."

I walked with him to the edge of the beach, hopped over the shrubs, and pointed down into the sandy pit. The fire circle remained in the center of the floor of the pit, but now I saw that the remains of a chicken dinner were scattered among the coals. I slid down into the hole, and kicked around in the sand to try and uncover the tin fuel can. It had disappeared.

"It's like a nest for someone or something," I said, trying not to shiver.

"This is your big discovery?" Ammie looked unimpressed when I nodded gravely.

"This is just a way station for the bootleggers. They've got to hide out during the day."

"Bootleggers? Prohibition is over," I reminded him.

"Yeah, but it's the same fellows who were bootlegging. Now they're running immigrants in from Canada. Bootleggers, smugglers. No difference."

"Smuggling immigrants?"

"Did you forget about our two Chinese friends?" Ammie walked away from the pit and back to the beach. I followed him, still resisting his explanation.

"Mr. Conawalski said there's some kind of crazy church over on the Canadian islands and they take these Chinese out on boats at night for some kind of ritual. He said those two must have fallen overboard in some kind of accident," I argued.

"He is pulling your leg, Augie Mohan. Lord, I don't see why. It's not like it's some horrible crime. Some Chinese want to get down to California and some Chinese in California want to get to Canada, and there's money to be had in helping 'em."

"Who pays?"

"They do, I guess. Or sometimes somebody who wants them for work pays."

"A lot of money?"

"Good money, very good money." Ammie rubbed his thumb and forefinger together knowingly. "But you'd never catch me doing that, no matter how much they offer."

"Why?"

"Well, who wants to do that? Live in pits during the day. Sleep in caves. Risk your boat and maybe a couple years of your life. They have put people in jail that got caught."

"Caves?"

"Well, wherever they can. Caves are better than the open air, I guess."

"How do you know about these smugglers, Ammie?" I asked. I wasn't sure what to believe now.

"I don't know. I'm not saying I met any. You just hear a lot of stuff in a barber shop. It's something I've always known was around. Nothing really that exciting. Not like being a real pirate."

I could picture the inscription on the bottom of the fuel can, with the name *Carolina* written in a scratchy, hurried hand. I wanted to tell Ammie about the discovery, but I couldn't produce the evidence and I was afraid he might think I was some kind of nervous Nellie, not fit for hiking through the woods on my own. Ammie was ready for more sawing, so we started again and worked until the mid-afternoon. The whole time I wrestled with this new information that Ammie had given me. I was relieved that Ammie's common sense explanation dispelled my fears of some supernatural being back from the dead, but the question of the *Carolina*'s fuel can was unresolved.

Ammie needed to go before it got to be too long past three o'clock when he would normally be home from school. He left off his side of the saw and turned to go, telling me he would come along on Saturday when we had his Pa's truck. I got up my courage and formed the question that had been bothering me all afternoon.

"Was Petesy Corrigan a smuggler? I found a fuel can from the *Carolina* in that pit."

"I guess it's possible. He was sneaky enough. But I pity those poor immigrants, even if they were just Chinese."

"Why?"

"My Pa says that Petesy was the kind of guy who was like the black cat. He had nine lives but if he crossed your path, it was bad luck for you," Ammie answered with a careless laugh.

I stood transfixed, looking at Ammie, but seeing my father walking up to Petesy's boat, stepping over a black cat sprawled in his way. It would have been the last time his feet touched land. When I said nothing in response, Ammie's face came to attention and his eyes registered embarrassment.

"I'm sorry, Augie. I'm sorry. I'm stupid. That was a stupid thing to say. I'm sorry to be talking about the dead that way. It was just barber shop talk. Just nonsense. People just say things to pass the time. I'm sorry for what happened to your Pa. And I'm even sorry for Petesy."

I believed him. Ammie was like a loose tree trunk in the waves. He didn't mean any harm; he just wasn't always in control.

"Get home before you get in trouble with your Pa," I called in a thick voice.

"See you Saturday?" Ammie called back, his face shadowed by regret.

"See you Saturday. Thanks."

Ammie trundled off toward Beacon Beach and home. I worked for the remainder of the afternoon, slowly hacking away at the next tree, and wondering why Mr. Conawalski would make up a tale about the Chinese when most of the adults in the town, including the sheriff, and maybe my Momma, seemed to know about the smugglers.

I finished my work and gathered my things well before sunset so that I could be on the road home before night fell. I had found only a small bit of relief in the fact that whoever might be using the beach as a campsite was real and still alive.

Fourteen

There's a Reason for the Pain

On Friday, the weather belied the season. The sun had the warmth of July, and the air, although somewhat musty with dried leaves, was sultry with the heat. I was glad that circumstances had conspired to give me this day in the open air. At Beacon Beach with our shirts off and our muscles working, Jim, Howard and I hoped the soft sea breeze would cool us off.

Momma had given us each a supply of potato biscuits, cheese, boiled eggs, some late pears, and a healthy portion of raisin pie. We wrapped the food and rolled it in some blankets that we tied with some cord and carried slung over our shoulders. I carried the saw and re-sharpened it at the cafe. Mr. O'Neill filled our water canteens and added some cooked chicken legs to our food supply. He loaned us a second saw and we walked the rest of the way out to the beach where we had decided to sleep the night so that when he arrived with the truck in the morning, everything would be cut and ready to load.

When I showed my brothers to the stretch of protected beach, Howard and Jim were surprised to see how much wood had already been cut. I told them about Ammie taking an afternoon off school to help, and made them swear not to mention it to anyone. Impressed, and heartened, they immediately set to the raft of trees still strewn across the beach and started sawing off rounds at a brisk pace.

We sawed, swam and ate throughout the day. The surf was calm, and with the protection of Tear Drop Point, that little inlet of water could almost have been mistaken for a lake, at least until we jumped into its chill. The cool was welcome, but we only needed a few minutes before we were glad to come back out on the beach and roll in our blankets to dry off.

As the afternoon ended, and night began to fall, I showed my brothers the hidden sand pit. They liked the idea of settling down for the night in that protected well since the air would start to cool to normal October temperatures once the sun went down. I had brought some matches and Howard was plenty pleased to start a campfire with sticks and the leftover coals.

We decided to eat slowly in order to save some of our food for the next day. We stuffed pieces of the chicken and bits of the cheese inside the biscuits and toasted them over the fire. Chewing slowly, we sat cross-legged on our blankets and talked. The conversation came around to how the two dead Chinese might have walked right past that very spot, and I told them that Ammie said the smugglers had probably dug the pit.

"You mean real smugglers have been here, where we're sitting right now?" asked Howard.

"It's possible," I answered. The fire crackled as it consumed the leaves and branches Howard had fed it.

"It's not a bad place to anchor," said Jim. "It drops off pretty sudden from the beach. I only went a little ways out before I couldn't touch bottom. A person wouldn't have to row too far to get in, and the boat would still be pulled into the cove where the water's quiet."

"So the two Chinese that Momma gave Last Rites to sat here once, and ate their dinner just like us," said Howard.

"The thing I don't understand," said Jim, "is that if they were here, someone brought them here. If someone brought them here, why would they jump in the water to try to swim away?"

"Especially if they were sick with the measles," said Howard.

"Either they were very scared of something, or they didn't know what they were doing or where they were and they fell in the water," guessed Jim.

"They could have been up on the top of the cliff, and something happened," I added.

I told them about finding the rope climb up to Shore Heights, and pulling myself up to the cave. Jim and Howard were incredulous.

"Go on!" Howard laughed. "That's a lie as big as a house."

"I'll show you tomorrow," I promised. "I'll show you and you can show Mr. O'Neill and Ammie when they come to help us."

"Next you'll be telling us that there's furniture and a piano and Chinese lanterns up there," Howard chortled.

"Is there anything up there?" Jim asked.

"I don't know because I didn't stay long enough to look around," I replied. "I was looking for trees and I saw everything on this beach, so I just went right back down and got to work."

"Why didn't you go back? I mean you've had a chance with all the days you've been here," Jim prodded.

I didn't want to admit the truth that I had been scared, but in the warmth of the campfire after an afternoon of shared hard work I couldn't hold back. I told them about the fuel container marked as belonging to the *Carolina* and the way it unnerved me.

"Until I talked to Ammie, I just wasn't sure why something from the *Carolina* would be showing up here. I didn't want to go back alone."

"So now you think the *Carolina* was a smuggler's boat, not a fishing boat?" asked Jim. "You're saying Pop worked as a smuggler?"

"Well, somebody from the *Carolina* has used this place. And now the fuel can is gone," I answered.

"All it means is somebody lifted the fuel can from the *Carolina*, and somebody else took it," said Howard. "Pop would not be involved in no smuggling."

"Augie, I think Howard's right. All it means is that someone uses this place. The *Carolina* fuel can could have gotten here a million different ways, and most of those ways are not really connected to the *Carolina*." Jim answered coolly, but I didn't hear real conviction in his voice.

We were thinking the same thing, I imagine. We were thinking that if a fuel can could wash up from a boat sunk miles away, bodies from that boat might wash up, too, and that event would be too horrible for us to stomach. We wrapped ourselves more tightly in our blankets to let the fire die out as we drifted off to sleep.

I thought about my brothers and how different we were from each other, but at the same time we had this one same thread that ran through us and linked us for forever. We had this same father who had left us, left us with his blood, his troubles, his anger and intelligence. We would always hear his voice in our memory, heeding it and fearing it at the same time. I guess what bound us was just knowing the same things. It made me think of the poem Jim thought was so important. I couldn't remember a word of it and I wanted to hear if it held the same peace of mind for me that it had given Jim.

"Jim," I murmured from within my blanket. "Jim, you awake?'

"Now, I am," he whispered back. "What?"

"Tell me that poem again, Jim, the one you told me at the hardware store."

"For God's sake," sighed Howard. "If we're going to start a poetry reading, maybe we should just all get up and dance a waltz together."

"You'll like it, Howard," said Jim. "You might even understand a word or two of it."

Howard's foot shot out from his blanket but only caught an empty corner of Jim's bed roll. Jim laughed.

"Go ahead, say your old poem. I'm not listening. I'm covering my ears," murmured Howard. I knew he wouldn't miss a word.

"It's like this," Jim began. "*Ah, as the heart grows older, it will come to such sights colder, by and by, not spare a sigh, though worlds of wanwood leafmeal lie, and yet you will weep and know why.*"

"Again," I ordered. He repeated it twice more and I said it again to myself.

"It's pretty," I said finally.

"It means there's a reason for the pain, and someday we'll understand it," Jim explained. I fell asleep with the rhythm of the poem marking my breathing in and out.

The next morning before dawn I awoke. Heavy dew had fallen, and I could feel the chill coming through my damp blanket through my clothes to my skin. Moving about in the dark to clamber up the side of the sand pit and into the bushes to relieve myself must have woken my brothers, and pretty soon the three of us were stretching and groaning and shaking off our blankets. We decided to get right to work because it was too cold to sit still. The idea of surprising Mr. O'Neill with a full load of rounds of firewood by early afternoon got us going fast. We weren't hungry yet, so we started sawing up the few trees that were left on the edge of the beach.

It was still gray although a weak light was beginning to seep around the corners of the cliffs behind us. Jim was working on the tree next to me, and Howard was on the other handle of Jim's saw.

The rip of the saw against the drier part of the tree, that wood beneath the outer bark, had a grating, chewing sound that filled the air around my head, so I didn't hear the boat at first. Now that I think back on it, that was probably a good thing, because if we had some warning— that is, if we had had some time to think about things—we probably wouldn't have done what we did.

Jim heard the noise first and stopped pushing the saw through the tree's core, and by necessity, Howard had to stop also.

"Hear that?" Jim asked.

"A boat's coming," answered Howard.

I interrupted the back and forth stroke of my saw to tell my brothers I could see right through their teasing joke, but the splash of oars made my head swivel towards the water. With the dark outline of Tear Drop Point looming like a ghost, the open skiff came into the cove. There were two passengers up front, and a rower handling the oars.

Crouched as we were over our respective trees, we were unnoticed by the pilot of the rowboat.

He brought the boat in toward the beach and began to approach the narrow sand shelf that jutted out underwater from that portion of the island. Pulling his oars in quickly to maneuver the prow across the sand bar, his cap fell back and I saw his red hair. Petesy Corrigan was landing! I could see it with my own eyes.

I started to run towards the water, shouting his name. Howard and Jim were behind me, leaping over tree trunks and calling out "Mr. Corrigan! Mr. Corrigan!" Petesy stood in the boat, startled for a moment, and the passengers grabbed the side of the boat to steady the rocking. Would he smile, I wondered, that toothy grin that had steadied so much of the rocking in his life, and explain that he and Pop had wandered off somewhere in Canada and were just now coming back, anxious to explain their mysterious trip? Would he clap me and my brothers on the back and apologize for all the unnecessary grief and worry their thoughtlessness had caused? Was one of those thin figures in the prow of the boat my Pop, home again and tired after all his hard work?

"Mr. Corrigan, where's Pop?" I heard Howard yelling behind me. "Where's Pop?" Howard's voiced strained with emotion and slipped out of his range into what sounded like the desolate screech of a gull.

Petesy had high rubber boots on, so he splashed heavily into the water when he jumped out of the boat. He didn't push the boat towards us over the sand bar as I had expected, however. Instead, he grasped the stern of the boat and started wheeling it around until the prow faced the open waters and Petesy could dig his boots into the sand bar for strength as he pushed the boat back into the sea.

We kept running, my brothers and I, into the water and over the sandy shallow bottom. I dove from the edge of the sandbar and was paddling furiously through the frigid water. Petesy had a head start and had gotten the boat off the bar, into the deep water, and he had pulled himself back in. He grabbed the oars and started stroking. Maybe he had gotten in two or three strokes before I caught up with him.

When I reached the boat, I took hold of the stern towards starboard and tried to hug the boat to me, to stop its forward progress. With no leverage but my own weight, the boat kept moving, dragging me along. Petesy lifted an oar out of its lock and slapped it down on my hand. The surprise viciousness of the attack made me let go, although I could feel he had done no real damage.

Just then, Jim and Howard reached the boat. They saw what Petesy had done with the oar, and Jim swiftly moved to the port of the boat, while Howard moved along the starboard in front of me. Petesy lifted the oar to swing at Howard's head and at just that moment Jim violently pulled the boat down towards him while I pushed up from my side. Howard's arm shot up and he grabbed the oar aimed at his head and pulled. Petesy went over the side headfirst. When he came up to the surface, he had a knife in his hand and he spoke for the first time.

"You boys go home," he yelled. "You don't know what you're into. Go home."

Howard had the oar and he jabbed it at Petesy. Petesy grabbed back but Howard was too fast and pulled the oar out of his reach.

"What are you doing out here, Petesy?" I asked, swimming up behind Howard. "And if you're here, where's Pop?"

"Go home," he yelled again. "Go home. Your Pop's gone. There's nothing we can do. Go home."

Howard lunged with the oar at Petesy's chest and this time Petesy pulled it free from Howard's grasp. Petesy banged it against the boat and one of the passengers, who had been huddled down in the stern lifted his head above the edge of the boat to see what caused the noise. Howard and I could see that the passenger was a young Chinese man. He took hold of the oar and hauled it into the boat.

"I'm getting into the boat now," said Petesy, "and I'm rowing back to the trawler. If you stop me, I will have to cut you."

The passenger held the oar at the ready to strike at our heads if we moved to touch Petesy. The cold water made our clothes heavy and our feet and legs, weighted down by our boots, were clumsy and slow. Howard started toward Petesy and extended his arm to grab hold of Petesy's hair or shirt. The blade in Petesy's hand glinted through the drops of water on it as he aimed it for Howard's hand. I reached down through the water and grabbed Howard's belt and pulled him back toward me. Petesy's knife sliced the air where Howard's hand would have been.

Petesy, with the knife in his hand, heaved his shoulders up over the side of the boat and the passenger bent over to hold on and to pull him in the rest of the way. Howard wrestled to be free of my hold, and I was confused about whether to attack Petesy or protect Howard. Howard broke away and we both started for Petesy when Jim's arm came out of the water and slung over Petesy's right ankle. Jim had been hiding behind the shadow of the stern waiting for the right moment to move. Petesy kicked but Jim's other hand came up and grabbed the other ankle. The man in the boat pulled on Petesy, and in his effort to hold on to the passenger, Petesy flung the knife in the water. Jim pulled himself upwards and in one swift movement braced his legs against the side of the boat and yanked Petesy back into the water.

A free-for-all began, with Jim reaching for a head hold, Howard grabbing his legs, and me trying to get his arms secured behind him. Jim and I were successful enough for Howard to undo Petesy's pants and pull them off with his boots. Meanwhile, the passenger took control of both oars and with short, swift strokes started to move the boat back out to the entrance to the cove, out to sea where presumably Petesy's trawler was anchored.

Snorting water, Howard swam towards shore with Petesy's clothing, while Jim yanked on Petesy's hair enough to convince him that we had the upper hand. Disarmed and half-naked, we pulled and pushed him to shore. As we stood him up on the sand bar and started to walk him to the beach, he made one more attempt to escape.

He wrenched away from our chilly fingers, but in bare feet he was no match for Howard, who raced over the pebbly beach behind him. Howard tackled him at a flying run, and the view of Howard's head hurtling toward Petesy's naked, skinny behind is a memory that still makes me smile.

We tied Petesy up with the rope from our bedrolls, and then we tied him to one of the fallen trees. We gathered enough wood to start a fire and dried off by it, all of us naked now and wrapped in blankets, our clothes and boots draped on rounds of wood stood on their side near the fire. Petesy was shivering a bit, but close enough to the fire to not freeze to death. We didn't have enough blankets for him to have one, and besides, we wouldn't have wanted to cover him up for fear his hidden hands would be able to untie the knots that held him. We ate our breakfast while Petesy watched and we talked about how surprised Mr. O'Neill would be to see that we had more to load in the truck than just firewood.

Jim got up the courage to ask Petesy again about Pop, but Petesy only cursed. By the time Mr. O'Neill arrived with Ammie and his father's truck, our clothes had toasted dry enough for us to put them back on. We untied Petesy from the tree, wrapped him in a blanket, and presented him to Mr. O'Neill like a runaway dog. Mr. O'Neill shook his head and said "Petesy, Petesy" as a way of greeting.

We loaded Petesy into the bed of the truck. Even Ammie wanted to ride with him, so Petesy had a guard of three boys staring in wonder at his drawn and tired face for the ride to the sheriff's office. I rode with Mr. O'Neill up front, glad to knead my fingers back to normal in the warmth of the cab.

"I could leave the boys here to keep on cutting while we drop Petesy off at the sheriff's," he offered.

"I doubt they'd stand for that. Howard might want to sleep at the sheriff's." I laughed a little to try and get some of my feelings out.

"Well, he is quite a discovery. Petesy Corrigan caught red-handed at last."

"So everybody knew what he was up to?"

"Mostly. But I thought he was a goner when the *Carolina* went down."

"So my Pop knew about Petesy?"

"Hard not to. The *Carolina* had one fishing net and it was rotted to shreds."

"You're saying my Pop was a smuggler." My mouth closed tight over the words.

"No, boy, no. Your Pop was a working man. He always paid his own way. A little dried out by this lovely Depression we've been enjoying lately, but as straight-arrow as any man made."

"But he was taking these Chinese..."

"He was navigating a boat," Mr. O'Neill broke in. He poked a finger at me in emphasis. "He wasn't the captain."

"He told us a lie was a lie."

"Did he happen to tell you how much he disliked hungry children?"

"I work. My brothers and me could always work."

"Of course you could. He knew it. He came in the day he left and asked about you."

"What did he say?"

"He asked if things were fine. I said of course they were. That you were an honest boy."

"What did he say then?"

"He said 'Damn right. He's my oldest son.'"

I looked away because the tears were burning to come out of my eyes, and I needed to wipe them with my sleeve. Mr. O'Neill whistled a bit, and asked a few questions about how we happened upon Petesy, but mostly he kept quiet.

So did Petesy, according to my brothers. He closed his eyes and rested his head on his knees, and never spoke, even when the sheriff gruffly pulled him off the bed and into the island jail.

A few hours later, after we had gone back and loaded up the wood, we stopped in the cafe for a hot lunch at Mr. O'Neill's insistence. Late in the afternoon, we pulled up in front of our house and it was clear the news had reached home before us. The sheriff's sedan was parked on the road, and a number of Momma's friends from church were at our gate. Momma broke into tears the moment she saw us. She jumped up from her chair and hugged us all, and it was the first moment I had really thought about having been in any danger.

As it turned out, finding Petesy brought up all the sadness again of Pop's death, but in a good way, a way I guess we needed. Petesy told the sheriff the story of what happened as soon as the sheriff threatened to turn Petesy over to the Coast Guard's officers. The sheriff brought the story to Momma, out of respect for her, so that she wouldn't hear it in pieces from the town's gossip mill.

Petesy, he said, had been running bootleg liquor from Canada to the States for years, so after Prohibition he just fell naturally into smuggling people, opium, money, or just about anything anybody wanted to move secretly across the border. Pop, and most everyone else that earned their living from the water knew it, but no police ever caught him with the evidence. Pop hadn't wanted to go to Vancouver Island on

Petesy's boat, but it was the only work available and we had been strapped for cash.

We all knew that Pop was mad that day that he left, but not, Momma said, because he had to go to work. He was mad that he had to do something dirty in order to do something right. He couldn't stand to see us hungry, but he couldn't bear Petesy's grin when he collected his money from starving immigrants, either.

"He wasn't a saint, God knows," said Momma. "And he did his fair share of drinking. But he wasn't a sneak or a cheat. The only thing that got him on Petesy's boat, he said, was the Depression."

Petesy anchored off the north part of Vancouver Island and rowed in to pick up the three Chinese men he planned to smuggle in to the San Juan Islands, and then later, on to Seattle. The storm came up fast, and he couldn't get back to the boat. Pop was out there alone. He had time to radio for help, but he couldn't handle the trawler in the rough seas. Petesy figures that he probably went on the deck to try to bring up the anchor, a job he was hardly built for, so he could move closer to shore, and got washed off by a wave. Without a pilot, the boat went down.

Petesy hid out for a while, and found another trawler where he was living in a small town near Vancouver. He repaired ship's hulls and engines and did some work for an old fisherman whose son had refused to take up fishing and moved into Vancouver. The man sold Petesy his boat on credit, and he was back in business. He made a few secret visits to our island because Mr. Conawalski was Petesy's silent partner, and Petesy needed cash for expenses. Besides, Petesy admitted, Tear Drop Point made a perfect hideout for his smuggled cargo.

The sheriff didn't stay for long, though we could have plied him with questions for hours longer. He had his hands full, he said, and had to get back to the jail. In two cells, he now had Petesy, the two Chinese they took off the trawler anchored off Tear Drop Point, Petesy's navigator and only other crew member, as well as Mr. Conawalski. My days of counting nails might be over, but so were his days of counting profits, legal and otherwise.

"All stuffed into a space meant for two at most," commented the sheriff. "And if that's not bad enough, of course I have Mrs. Conawalski camped outside the cell and giving advice to any and all of the prisoners, except her husband, who won't even look at her."

"But you can do me a favor, Augie," the sheriff continued. "Tomorrow, come into to my office and help me out with something. You and I have something to investigate."

"Me? What can I do?" I stuttered.

"Ammie Kilgore tells me you found a way up to Shore Heights," he prodded me. "You can show me that, as well as help me find my way around Mr. Conawalski's store. I think there's probably some records of transactions there that I should know about."

My brothers looked at me admiringly, as though some of the transgressions of my past might be at long last forgotten.

Epilogue

Still no one knows exactly what happened to the two young Chinese that washed up on the shores. Of course, neither Petesy nor Mr. Conawalski admitted much of anything. It is one thing to go to jail for a few years for smuggling like both of them did, and quite another to be implicated in a death. No, Wally and Petesy said nothing at their trials about having smuggled or even spoken to the Chinese couple. There were lots of smugglers in the area, they maintained, and they were probably part of some other deal gone bad.

The sheriff could not produce enough evidence to prove otherwise, so Petesy and Wally spent a few years in the federal penitentiary in San Francisco for violating customs and immigration laws. Mr. Conawalski probably suffered the most because he had to leave his daughters in the care of his confused and broken wife. They sold the hardware store and moved to Seattle, where Mrs. Conawalski had family. The girls, I'm told, got jobs in a shoe factory and married young. Petesy contracted hepatitis while he was in prison and died just a year after he got out.

We had our own explanation, the sheriff and I, for what had happened to the couple. We had found some clothing for a male and a female, along with blankets, stashed in the cave inside a small canvas bag. The bag still held a sack of dried fruit and rice cakes wrapped in paper. There was a Bible in English and some kind of little pamphlet in Chinese. Folded inside the Bible was a marriage certificate signed and dated just a week before they washed ashore. It was from a Catholic church in Vancouver, and when the sheriff talked to the priest there he remembered the couple well.

"They were scared, but they were sincere, and they were old enough to know what they wanted," Father Kelly from St. Brendan's told him. "I married them with just my altar boys as witnesses, because the young man told me she was pregnant. He was going to work, he said, in San Francisco, and everything would be fine. I'm sorry to hear it didn't turn out that way."

We figured that Petesy, or maybe some other smuggler, told the Chinese to hole up there at Tear Drop Point, until they could be taken on the next leg of the trip. But Petesy's plans went awry, and without knowing what to do, they were left to fend for themselves in a cold cave.

About a week after the sheriff came back from Vancouver and closed the investigation, on a Sunday afternoon a Chinese gentleman in a handsome suit and glossy leather shoes presented himself at the sheriff's home. They talked for a while, and the sheriff drove the gentleman, Mr. Chu, out to our house. He was, he explained to us in correct but slightly accented English, the father of the man whose name appeared on the marriage certificate.

He was carrying the canvas bag with their few remaining things, which the sheriff had given him. He wanted, he said, to go to their graves and bury the marriage certificate with his son. He thought his son would like to have it back. He asked if Momma would come, since the sheriff had said she was the one who had given them their Last Rites.

"Did you know the woman?" Momma asked Mr. Chu as gently as she could.

"I knew of her. She was poor. An orphan some uncle had sent to Canada to work waiting tables. Not an honorable position but she met my son and fell in love. I told him he couldn't marry her."

"So he decided to elope," Momma added.

"I didn't know about any baby. We said we would buy her ticket home to China," he answered. After a long moment, he added, "It was a mistake."

"They were peaceful together, that's how I saw them," Momma said. She sat down at the kitchen table and motioned Mr. Chu to sit also.

He sank into the chair next to her, and the hand holding the marriage certificate started to shake. Momma put her hand over his hand.

"They could have come home. They had to know I would only be angry a little while. They could have come home," he said. His hand went to his face and covered his eyes. His shoulders started to heave.

"They are home, Mr. Chu," said Momma quietly. "They are home, just like Augie's Pop here went home. We'll be there, too, someday. You'll see your son again."

"They could be here now. I could see him now if I had only understood." Mr. Chu cried these words into his hands. Momma looked up at the sheriff for guidance.

The sheriff sat down and put his arm over Mr. Chu's back. I sat on the other side of the table. It took a while for Mr. Chu to stop heaving and shaking. Finally, he straightened up and the sheriff withdrew his arm. Momma nodded and the sheriff started to talk.

"She died, Mr. Chu. It wasn't your fault. They met up with some bad people, she picked up the measles, and she died in that cave. That's what we think. They had food. They had shelter. They could have stayed up there and waited for their smugglers to come back, or they could have gone for help. But she died, and their baby died, and he must have been crazy in his grief, and probably in a fever. He did what he thought was right and died with them."

Mr. Chu laid the marriage certificate out in front of him, and smoothed it flat on the table. Slowly, he ran his finger over the names of his son and daughter-in-law, once and again, in a tender gesture.

"He was a good son," he said simply, looking up at Momma.

"And so he was a good man. He loved her, and he acted out of love," Momma answered. "That's all you can ask for, for that love that everybody gives in their own way. And all we can do is answer with our own love."

Momma rode with the sheriff to the cemetery and the unmarked grave where the young couple lay side by side in one grave. She said Mr. Chu buried the marriage certificate right where their hearts would be.

The next Sunday I hiked out to Beacon Beach, climbed up to the cave at Shore Heights but what everybody now called China Rock, and as hard as I could I heaved a corked bottle from the mouth of the cave into the ocean. Inside the bottle was a picture of Pop and me that had been taken years before. He was laughing, laughing at me as I bobbled a big ice cream cone he had just bought me at the fair in Anacortes. Maybe part of the laugh was mean, but somewhere in that laugh was some love, and I thought maybe that bottle would find Pop and be with him until I could get there.

Author's Note

The China Rock legend was first related to me by Bergen Wagner, a friend of our then teenaged son, Isaac. Bergen spent many summers with his family biking and sailing in the San Juan Islands in the northwest corner of Washington State. I imagine he heard the story in one of the local marinas where he listened to the adults spin their tales.

He told us the story because he knew we loved the San Juans and wanted to know as much as possible about their history. Bergen's version took place in the mid-19th century, and in it China Rock was an island unto itself, consisting of one very large rock. My re-telling is quite different, a confabulation of his history with my imagination. I am grateful though for his sharing it on that winter's afternoon, as I am grateful to Gerard Manley Hopkins for Jim's poem which Hopkins called "Spring and Fall".

I would also like to thank the kind stewards of the San Juan Historical Museum for allowing me access to their newspaper archives, to Lopez Islanders, Anne and David Hall, who were most encouraging readers, to Jim Thomsen a careful and caring editor, to Kristie Robb, a priceless critic, and to Paul Robb, who makes me smile.

Laura Kelly Robb
Seattle, Washington
March, 2013

Discussion Questions for *China Rock*

1. What is the role of similarities and differences within a family and between siblings? Are siblings closer in age apt to be more compatible than siblings separated by more than a couple years? Which differences are minor and which are major when it comes to sibling compatibility?

2. How does the immigrant experience in the U.S. differ for different ethnicities? What impact, if any, does the perception of the immigrant by U.S. residents have on the experience?

3. What are the advantages and disadvantages of growing up in a small town? Has the small town influenced the view of adulthood of Augie and his siblings? What difference, if any, has living in a small town on a small island made in the lives of the Mohans?

4. What does Augie learn about Pop Mohan after his disappearance? How does this new perspective alter your view of Pop's role as father?

5. What is the role of religion in the Mohans' life? What is the role of faith?

6. What considerations do you think Momma had when making the decision to keep Jim in school? In the Mohans' situation, what do you think would be the fairest decision? Would Momma's considerations be the same in the case of Howard's leaving school?

7. Do any of the characters show noticeable growth during the story? Do any diminish in their humanity or moral strength?

8. Jim seems deeply disappointed with Augie's failure to tell the truth. Does Jim expect too much from Augie? Has Augie learned anything from Jim? How would the Mohans' situation be better or worse if Augie had consistently told the truth?

9. This story takes place during the Great Depression of the 1930's. What would be different if the story happened now? What conditions might be the same?

10. At one point, Augie insists that it is his right to make his own mistakes. Does good parenting mean letting offspring pursue their own path, despite the parents' misgivings? How should we judge Pop's harsh attitude towards his children's behaviors and accomplishments?

Made in the USA
San Bernardino, CA
28 April 2013